"I'm pretty sure

Andy's expressio
disappeared. "Yes, ...

His frank acknowledgment took Desiree aback. "That's flattering, Andy, but—"

"Cards on the table. Are you or are you not attracted to me?"

She took a slow breath and let it out. "I suppose I am, but—"

"That's all I need to know." He shoved back his chair and stood. "Let's put that playhouse together."

"Wait." She got up, too. "It's not that simple."

"The playhouse or us?"

"Us. It's complicated. *I'm* complicated. Even though I'm attracted to you, we wouldn't be a good fit."

"I'm aware you're complicated. That's one of your best qualities. I'm also aware you've had a lot of guys in your life and you haven't stuck with any of them. That makes you a risky proposition."

"Exactly! You'd be nuts to get involved with me. Since I care about you, I should never have flirted with you a while ago."

"Did you enjoy it?"

"That's not the point."

"It's the whole point."

HEATING UP THE COWBOY'S CHRISTMAS

ROWDY RANCH

Vicki Lewis Thompson

Ocean Dance Press

HEATING UP THE COWBOY'S CHRISTMAS
© 2023 Vicki Lewis Thompson

ISBN: 978-1-63803-929-7

Ocean Dance Press LLC
PO Box 69901
Oro Valley, AZ 85737

This is a work of fiction. Any resemblance to
actual persons, living or dead, business
establishments, events, or locales is entirely
coincidental.

Visit the author's website at
VickiLewisThompson.com

Want more cowboys? Check out these other titles by Vicki Lewis Thompson

Rowdy Ranch
Having the Cowboy's Baby
Stoking the Cowboy's Fire
Testing the Cowboy's Resolve
Rocking the Cowboy's Christmas
Roping the Cowboy's Heart
Tempting the Cowboy's Sister
Craving the Cowboy's Kiss
Heating Up the Cowboy's Christmas

The Buckskin Brotherhood
Sweet-Talking Cowboy
Big-Hearted Cowboy
Baby-Daddy Cowboy
True-Blue Cowboy
Strong-Willed Cowboy
Secret-Santa Cowboy
Stand-Up Cowboy
Single-Dad Cowboy
Marriage-Minded Cowboy
Gift-Giving Cowboy

The McGavin Brothers
A Cowboy's Strength
A Cowboy's Honor
A Cowboy's Return
A Cowboy's Heart
A Cowboy's Courage
A Cowboy's Christmas
A Cowboy's Kiss
A Cowboy's Luck

1

Andy Hartmann scanned the text that had popped up on his computer screen at eleven-sixteen on Friday morning.

The log cabin playhouse came after all! We can assemble it in Rowdy Roost, but we're short on time. Will you ask Jess if she and Beau can come over tonight and help? We'll put Mav to bed before we start.

Christmas was on Monday. The holiday edition of *The Wagon Train Sentinel* was due at the printers by noon and he hadn't finished his editorial.

But he would never ignore a text from Desiree Annabelle McLintock. Well, maybe if the building caught fire. But even then....

He typed a quick reply. *I'm available tonight. I'll check with Jess. Are you sure we can get it out of Rowdy Roost?*

I measured and it'll fit through the double doors we used to move in the bar and the pool table. Come for dinner. Six o'clock. Invite Jess, Beau and Mav, too, of course.

Of course. Their group of five was a social unit tied together by a red-headed little bundle of joy named Maverick — his granddaughter. And Desiree's.

He closed out the text exchange. *I'll let them know.*

And he would, even though a traitorous voice in his head urged him to flip the script on this plan.

Desiree had shown him the DIY playhouse online back in September. He'd happily agreed to split the cost and help her put it together as a Christmas present for Mav.

The project had everything going for it. They'd create a unique gift that their granddaughter wouldn't outgrow anytime soon, and they'd spend time alone while they constructed it.

He'd been looking for that opportunity. Once Mav had made her appearance fourteen months ago, he and Desiree had been thrown together constantly. But they were always in a crowd.

In the early days, he'd been fine with that. Although the pain of losing Mary had eased after seven years, that didn't mean he was on the hunt. Just the opposite. He liked his own company and he'd settled into a comfortable routine that suited him. Until fourteen months ago.

Regular contact with Desiree McLintock would affect any man with a pulse. He'd seen guys half her age take notice, but she seemed to have given up dating, at least recently. That was one of many things that fascinated him. And challenged him, damn it.

She was a puzzle, a woman who'd had many men in her life but hadn't seen fit to marry any of them. He wanted to know why. Asking her would require a private conversation, a deeper connection.

She liked him well enough, but he couldn't get a bead on whether she'd be open to more than friendship. Did he dare ask her out and risk rejection? What about the awkwardness that would likely follow if she turned him down? So far he'd held off.

Building a playhouse over the course of several evenings would have been a perfect setup — not a date, but an opportunity to find out what happened when they spent hours alone in her house. Shipping bottlenecks had blasted that idea to smithereens.

A timer pinged on his computer. Eleven-thirty. He sighed and returned to his editorial, typing fast. He'd make the deadline, no problem. He was a newspaperman. He ate deadlines for breakfast.

Twenty minutes later, Jess appeared in the doorway of his office. She'd worn the Christmas-green sweater he'd bought her last year because it exactly matched her eyes and green was her favorite color.

She'd been working with him for more than two years and he still had to pinch himself. He'd never have predicted she'd leave her job back East. What a dream come true. "I'm done. Just let me check the last paragraph, see if it works."

"No rush. We have nine whole minutes left."

"Oh, well, then. I have time to read through the rest of—"

"Dad."

"Just teasing you, kiddo." He skimmed the last paragraph, changed one word and sent it off to Monica. "Done."

Jess glanced over her shoulder toward their small newsroom. "Got it?"

"Dropping it in, now," Monica called out. "Aaaand… it's a wrap! Party time at the Buffalo!

Jess swung back to him, her expression animated. "Beau texted a few minutes ago. He's on his way to town with Mav. She can't wait to see her Grandy."

"And I can't wait to see her. Say, would you please ask Monica and Joe to head over and grab us a table? I have something quick to discuss with you. Christmas stuff."

"You bet. Want them to order for us? I'm just getting a burger and fries."

"Me, too. Yeah, if they'd order that would be wonderful."

"Be right back." She hurried away.

Shutting down his computer, he shoved his glasses to the top of his head and rolled back his chair.

"They'll handle it." Jess came back in and rested a hip on the edge of his desk. "What Christmas stuff?"

"The playhouse showed up today."

"It *did*? Wow, that's cutting it close. Will you guys have time to put it together?"

"Desiree thinks we need help, so she wondered if you and Beau could come over for dinner tonight and lend us a hand."

"What about Mav? You don't want her to see it, right?"

"We'd start after we put her to bed."

"Okay. I'll check with Beau, but I think we can make it."

He gazed at her. "I figured you could, but I almost hoped you'd have a conflict."

Her eyes widened. "Oh, *really*." Then she smiled. "I wondered if this moment would ever come."

"If the shipment hadn't been stuck on a container ship in Long Beach I wouldn't be in this position."

"Are you telling me this project was all about spending time alone with Desiree?"

"*No*, it was about building a cool gift for Mav which tangentially would allow me to spend time alone with Desiree."

"You could have told me you wanted a chance to be alone with her. Beau and I would have been happy to arrange—"

"Yeah, and she would have caught on that you were maneuvering. I don't want machinations. The playhouse would have been subtle. Perfect."

"No worries. I'll come up with a conflict."

"Nope, that's dishonest. I have two choices — abandon the idea or man up and admit to her I want just the two of us to work on it."

"She might be flattered."

"Or she might think I'm an idiot and insist on having you and Beau help. There's the possibility we won't get the damn thing finished if we do it by ourselves."

Her smile widened into a grin. "Because you'll get distracted?"

"No, because those *some assembly required* projects can be a nightmare. Everyone knows that. The smart thing is for all four of us to tackle it and get 'er done."

"But then you lose your golden opportunity."

He took a deep breath and let it out. "Yes, ma'am." He rolled back his chair and stood. "We should get going. Beau and Mav could be there by now." Walking over to the coat tree in the corner, he unhooked his Stetson and his heavy jacket. "I'll make a decision after lunch."

Icy patches on the sidewalk made the walk from the *Sentinel* office to the Buffalo treacherous and Andy resisted the urge to take Jess's arm. She was at least as capable of navigating the terrain as he was and maybe even better at it. A time might come when she took *his* arm.

But until that day arrived, his protective instincts would keep surfacing. Being her only remaining parent could have something to do with that.

A wreath on the tavern's antique door and Christmas lights in the windows facing the street gladdened his heart every year. He never got tired of Christmas.

He held the door for Jess and she walked past the large wooden buffalo at the entrance. This year the buffalo's greeting changed daily. Today it moaned *Get yoouur hollyyyy jollyyyy onnnn.*

Jess glanced back as he triggered the sensor and the buffalo repeated the message. "Have you figured out who records those?"

"I could if I tried, but then what? I'm not going to publish a spoiler and ruin the fun of the mystery."

She took off her coat. "You know, don't you?"

"Nope."

"Okay, if you say so." She scanned the room and waved to Beau, who stood and beckoned them over to the table where Monica and Joe were already sipping mugs of cider and Mav was ensconced in a highchair.

At Andy's request, the highchair was routinely tucked in beside the empty seat he planned to take. His granddaughter was in full cuteness mode, playing peek-a-boo with Monica and giggling as Joe balanced a spoon on his nose.

But when Andy slid onto his chair, she focused all her attention on him. He returned the favor, leaning in so she could pat his cold cheeks and he could give her a kiss on her little button nose. That always made her laugh.

"Looks like we've been benched, Joe," Monica said.

Jess laughed. "Don't feel like the Lone Ranger. Once this guy shows up, she has no time for Beau or me, either. Right, Dad?"

"Mostly, but she'll toss me over in a heartbeat if Desiree's around." He gazed into green eyes so like Jess's at that age. "Won't you, kiddo?"

"Gaa—dy!" She couldn't quite say Grandy, the nickname Desiree had chosen for him, but she had the *G* and the *dy* down.

When the food arrived, Mav insisted on sharing her fries with him, but only after she'd thoroughly mauled each one by squeezing it between her chubby fingers and reshaping it like a piece of clay. Once it passed muster, she'd lean toward him and drop it carefully on his plate.

She watched to make sure he ate the food she'd provided. Ignoring the conversation going on among the other adults at the table, he polished off every single mangled fry until she'd given him all she had.

He handed over one of his.

She beamed at him as if he was her star pupil. Then she slowly ate it.

"Now you've done it, Andy," Beau said. "You'll never eat your fries in peace again."

"And why would I want to? That's boring." He gave her another one, dancing it across the tray.

She grinned, displaying her small teeth, four on top and two on the bottom. Then she took the fry and gave him a sly look, as if they shared a secret. Jess used to do that.

His chest warmed with love for this beautiful little grandchild. Guaranteed she'd run into her new playhouse on Christmas morning squealing with excitement.

Okay, it was decided. He'd ask Beau and Jess for help with it. Getting it finished on time was more important than his half-baked plan for alone time with Desiree.

Everyone ordered a slice of the Buffalo's famous chocolate layer cake for dessert. Mindful of Mav's holiday outfit, Andy fed her bites of his instead of letting her have a chunk to herself.

Although she was clearly annoyed at being denied a plate and a fork, the chocolate restored her good humor. She cheerfully waved goodbye to Joe and Monica when they left to do some last-minute shopping.

"That was fun." Jess tucked her napkin under her plate. "Thanks for managing the cake part, Dad."

"Chocolate frosting would be tough to get out of that sweater."

"Isn't it cute? Love those snowflakes."

"My mom bought it for her when they went shopping last week, " Beau said.

"What a surprise."

"Speaking of surprises…" Jess gave him a look. "Have you made a decision about you-know-what?"

"Yep. I'd like you and Beau to help with it."

Beau pushed back his plate. "Help with what?"

"Your mother texted me this morning. The pl—" He caught himself and glanced at Maverick, who understood way more words than she could speak. "Hey, kiddo, let's get you out of there, okay?" Leaving his seat, he extricated her from the highchair while Jess quietly explained to Beau that Mav's big gift had finally arrived.

"I'm surprised she didn't say anything when she called me about my dad's visit. It must have shown up after that."

"Your dad's visit?"

Just what Andy wanted to ask. He sat down with Mav on his lap. The subject of Desiree's ex-lovers made him twitchy.

"He contacted Mom this morning and asked if he could arrive sometime between Christmas and New Year's."

"Wow, that's unexpected. When he came to see Mav last year, I got the impression he wouldn't be back for quite a while. I wasn't even sure he had a good time."

"I thought the same," Andy said, "but you must be tickled about it, son." He did his best to sound enthusiastic for Beau's sake.

"I am, although it's short notice. And he wants to stay out at Rowdy Ranch this time instead at the hotel like he did last year."

"I guess Mav can sleep in our room," Jess said, "and we'll haul the guest bed out of storage."

"Actually, he told Mom he didn't want to put Maverick out of her room. He was calling to ask if he could stay at the ranch house, instead. To make it easier on our new little family."

Tension gathered at the base of Andy's skull. Desiree would likely agree if it meant her precious granddaughter could stay in her own room.

"Oh." Jess looked across the table, her gaze assessing. She likely could guess what he was thinking. Breaking eye contact, she turned back to her husband. "This holiday is a big deal for your mom. I think your dad should stay with us."

"I agree. I could tell she wasn't in love with the idea of him staying at the house, especially since it's last minute. She didn't give him an answer. Told him she'd think about it. I emphasized we'd be happy to set him up in Mav's room."

"Absolutely."

"So, Andy." Beau glanced at him. "What were you saying about wanting us to help with the… project?"

"Your mother wants to start tonight after dinner and asked me to enlist you guys, but she and I can handle it. I'm sure you have plenty of other things to do."

"Hey, no worries. If you guys need a hand, we can make the time to—"

"We could," Jess said, "but we're not going to."

"Why not?"

"I'll explain it to you later. We need to take this munchkin home for a nap and Dad has stuff to do."

"Okay, but listen, Andy, if you and Mom get in a pickle, give us a call. We'll bundle up the kid and ride to the rescue."

He swallowed a laugh. "I'll keep that in mind, son."

2

After a busy morning wrapping gifts, Desiree enjoyed a relaxed lunch with Marybeth and Buck in the ranch house kitchen. While she and Marybeth lingered over coffee, Buck left to check the watering system in the barn. Snow was in the forecast and he wanted to make sure the heating element was working.

"I'm glad you invited Beau and Jess to come help with that playhouse tonight." Marybeth got up and fetched the coffee carafe, her long gray braid swaying gently as she walked to the counter and back. She refilled each of their mugs without asking. After thirty-plus years, certain things were understood. "I'd offer, but then Buck would insist on lending a hand, and he's—"

"That would be ridiculous after all the hard work he does during the day." Desiree smiled her thanks for the coffee. "I wouldn't expect that of him. Or you." Marybeth was a pint-sized Energizer Bunny who'd never admit to being tired.

"Then I'll cook dinner for you guys. I can do that much."

"I appreciate the offer, but you need to go home and have a quiet evening with Buck like you planned. I'll make something easy. They'll pitch in. They always do."

"But then I won't get to see Mav."

"Not for long. She'll be hustled off to bed right after dinner so we can get to work."

"True."

"You'll be seeing a lot of her starting Sunday night."

"Also true." Marybeth picked up her mug and took a sip. "Good thing Steven didn't ask to come this weekend."

"He probably figured out that would be pushing it. You can't just invite yourself to come for Christmas when it's only a couple days away."

"He showed up out of the blue when he came to see Maverick last year, too. Is that his pattern?"

"I have no idea since that was the first time he'd set foot in Wagon Train since he left thirty years ago. I didn't appreciate him doing that then, either, but it was September, not right before a major holiday."

"Have you decided whether to let him stay here?"

"No, but I'd rather he didn't." She sighed. "On the other hand, I hate the thought of Jess and Beau hauling all Mav's stuff into their room. The crib will fit, but not the cute little tree that she helped decorate. She loves that thing."

"Not to mention dragging their guest bed out of storage. Could you farm him out to one of the others?"

"I'm sure they'd do it if I asked, but that's not fair. And he won't arrive until the twenty-sixth, so the major stuff will be over."

"How long does he plan to stay?"

"He didn't say and I didn't ask. I should have, but I was scrambling to think how to respond. It would be great if he and Beau could build a relationship, but—"

"You don't want him hanging around the house."

"Right."

Marybeth gave her a long look. "Do you suppose he's hoping to share your—"

"Oh, no. I made that clear. If I agree he can stay with me, he'll get the twin in Beau's old room. He said it would be fine."

"Because he expects to sweet-talk you into changing your mind?"

"I wouldn't put it past him. He sounded different on the phone. I'll bet dollars to donuts he's had his fill of traveling and imagines rekindling the flame and settling in here." She made a face, which got a laugh out of Marybeth.

"C'mon. You must have loved him at some point."

"Of course I did. He had a lot of good points, but he was no Charley Fox."

"Aw, honey, you say that about all of them."

"I know. I might be idealizing him a little, but so does his widow. Everyone at the Buckskin Ranch adored—" She caught herself.

Marybeth had patiently listened to variations on this theme several times over the past two years. Time to give it a rest.

The bittersweet trip had been essential. Until she'd visited Apple Grove and the Buckskin Ranch, she hadn't known for sure if she'd done the right thing by keeping her pregnancy a secret from Charley.

He'd never found out. She'd quietly moved to Wagon Train and given birth to Sky. Eventually she'd told Sky about his father and he'd chosen not to connect.

Bottom line, Charley had married the woman he loved. He'd lived the life he'd wanted and now he was gone. End of story.

She took a deep breath. "I need to stop talking about him."

"That's up to you. I'll keep listening if it helps you."

"It did. It has, and I appreciate your patience, but it's time to let go. I'll stick a pin in it after I say it one last time. Charley Fox really was one in a million."

"I'm sure he was." Marybeth grinned. "But that still leaves you with the issue of Steven, who's very much alive and looking for a second chance."

That made her laugh. "Don't worry. I'll disabuse him of that right off the bat, but I don't want to give him the bum's rush, either. If he and Beau could become closer, that would be fabulous. Technically he's Mav's grandfather, too."

"I wish him luck with that one. Andy has the position all sewn up."

"That's for sure. He—" Her phone chimed. "Speak of the devil." Leaving the table, she grabbed her phone from the kitchen counter and put it in speaker mode. "What's up?"

"I talked to Jess and Beau."

His deep baritone had a hesitant note she seldom heard. "Can they make it?"

"They can, but..." He took a breath. "I'd like for us to put it together, just you and me."

"You would?" She blinked and looked over at Marybeth to get her reaction. Tough to say because she'd ducked her head. She might be laughing.

"It'll be more significant if we're the only ones who work on it, since it's from us."

"Mav doesn't have to know we had help."

"No, but... let's just say it's important to me."

"It's important to me that we get it finished. I don't want to present her with a partially completed playhouse on Christmas morning."

"We won't. I'm confident we can do this."

She paused to check on Marybeth. Yep, definitely giggling. "Alrighty, then. If you're confident, I'm confident. Are you still coming for dinner?"

"How about if I bring it? I made a big batch of vegetable soup yesterday and I even made bread."

"From scratch?"

"In the bread maker. Tastes pretty good."

"Sounds terrific. I have Christmas cookies for dessert."

"Excellent."

"Six o'clock? Is that still good?"

"How about a little sooner? Unless you have things to do. I'm not going back to the office, so—"

"I've wrapped up most of what I had to accomplish today. Come around four, then, and we'll get a head start, then break for dinner."

"Perfect."

"See you soon." She disconnected and turned to Marybeth. "All right, all right, I know what you're thinking, but—"

"And you're not thinking the same thing? Could he be more obvious?"

"No. But I hope to hell we can put that thing together in the amount of time we have left."

"Of course you will. Unless..." She cracked up again.

"Unless *nothing.* This is Andy we're talking about. He's a perfect gentleman. It's not like he's going to try and seduce me." Her stomach fluttered.

"Who knows? You might decide to seduce him. And don't pretend you haven't thought about it."

"I've thought about it. Dismissed it."

"Why?"

"What if the sex is awful?"

Marybeth rolled her eyes. "You wouldn't let that happen."

"Well, no, I'd make sure we both had fun, but I don't want to find out he's boring in bed. That's what I meant by awful. I'm probably better off sticking with my fantasies."

"Oh, really? You fantasize about him?"

"Sometimes. His editorials are good."

"His *editorials*?" Marybeth got the giggles again. "Only you would be turned on by well-crafted prose."

"He's a good writer! He comes across as funny, kind, intelligent, which he is, and—"

"He also has a good body, but I suppose you haven't—"

"I've noticed." Her stomach fluttered again. "But that doesn't mean he's a good lover."

"At least he'd look good naked."

"Marybeth!" She blushed. "Stop it!"

"It's obvious he has a big—"

"Hey!"

"*Crush*! I was gonna say *crush*."

"Sure you were. Anyway, big crush or big whatever, if we had mediocre sex that would ruin everything. I'm not doing it."

3

Lazy snowflakes settled on the windshield of Andy's truck as he bumped along Rowdy Ranch's dirt road and thought about Beau's father. The guy — what was his name? Oh, who cared. The point was, he had ulterior motives.

A good newsman could spot ulterior motives a mile away. The part about not wanting to put Mav out of her bedroom was brilliant, because it was true.

No decent grandfather would want to displace her, especially if they'd watched her face when she turned on the lights in the small Christmas tree in her room. Every night it was an event.

This guy hadn't seen that, but he could assume Maverick's comfort was an ace in his pocket. By playing it, he could hit the jackpot of several nights in Desiree's house.

Nobody would question his motives — nobody but the guy who understood why a man would want to score those nights under Desiree McLintock's roof. Then again, was he projecting because *he* had ulterior motives?

He couldn't deny it. Up to now he'd been slow-playing this situation, building a foundation for what might eventually become something really cool.

Wouldn't you just know it? When he finally had an opening, along comes this other grandpa who invites himself to stay awhile with the woman he used to have regular sex with. That gave the dude a huge advantage. He was a proven commodity. Dammit to hell.

The truck lurched and he almost bit his tongue. Must have stomped on the gas and hit a rut going too fast. As light faded from the sky, his truck's headlights revealed the washboard effect created by winter storms and freezing temperatures. He needed to slow down.

The bouncy ride reminded him of sitting a trot, something he hadn't mastered yet. Could Grandpa #2 sit a trot without looking like a bobblehead doll? If so, that gave him another advantage.

When Grandpa #2 had swooped in more than a year ago, Andy had possessed no riding skills. His first ride had happened on Angie's birthday, when his horse had wandered into the barn with him on board. He'd come close to getting knocked out cold.

Since then he'd been on several trail rides. They were always a family affair that included him, Desiree, Jess, Beau and Mav, who rode in a carrier on Beau's back. Desiree had never suggested a ride with just the two of them.

In fact, she'd made no attempt to see him alone, ever. He had no reason to believe she'd ordered the playhouse with that plan in mind. All indications pointed to a depressing conclusion — she'd never considered him as a potential lover.

And yet, at times she'd glanced at him with a gleam in those gorgeous hazel eyes, as if... nah, he'd be a fool to attach significance to such moments. If she'd wanted to start something, she would have. Desiree was many things, but *shy* wasn't one of them.

Clearly Grandpa #2 wasn't shy, either, since he'd boldly invited himself to stay with her, initiating forced proximity. Oh, yeah, the guy knew exactly what he was doing.

He'd stayed away for years. Why show up now? Because he wanted Desiree back. Tucked into that house with her, he had a shot at reigniting the flame. He knew things, private things that Andy didn't.

Frustration gripped him, tightening his jaw. Unless he grabbed his chance in the next few days, he could lose her forever.

But he couldn't just make a move. He had no basis for it. Without some leadup, flirting and so on, he might scare the hell out of her, maybe even get himself slapped. He needed more time, more wiggle room. Instead he had a deadline.

Deadlines didn't bother him when it came to putting words on a page. He met each one with cool confidence. Could he do the same with this situation? Maybe. He could start by calming the hell down.

Yeah, right. The moment her spectacularly decorated house came into view, his heart raced and his breath caught.

Multicolored lights twinkled in the trees, along the porch and even on a large wreath hung above the barn door. Matching five-foot Christmas trees sat on either side of the front entrance.

He'd participated in the day-long event that had created this wonderland. He'd hung lights, attached garlands, and trimmed trees alongside Desiree and the rest of the family.

Her enthusiasm for life drew him like a moth to flame. Whenever he was with her, he could almost taste it. He yearned to be immersed in her world — mentally, physically, spiritually.

Parking the truck, he switched off the engine and sat for a moment, gathering his forces. This was only Friday. He had until Tuesday, the twenty-sixth, to convince Desiree he was a better bet than Beau's dad.

Three full days and four nights. He'd make the most of them.

Climbing out of the warm cab, he welcomed the frigid breeze as he fetched the soft-sided cooler from the passenger seat and headed toward the porch. Two mason jars filled with soup, one quart each, clinked against each other with each step.

Snowflakes landed on the shoulders of his shearling coat and his black Stetson. His Tony Lamas crunched the frozen ground under his feet. He wasn't a cowboy, but he made no apology for dressing like one. He'd always liked the look.

Unfortunately, as he'd learned last September, so did Grandpa #2. And pulled it off, too.

Taking a deep, calming breath, he climbed the steps. The wreath on the door, the trees on either side and the pine boughs on the railing made the porch smell like Christmas.

Desiree opened the door before he reached it. "There you are, punctual as always."

There was nothing wrong with being labeled punctual. It just didn't sound very sexy. "And there you are, welcoming as always." He'd chosen *welcoming* on purpose. Starting the evening by complimenting her looks would be cheesy, especially when she'd clearly chosen old clothes she could work in.

But Desiree McLintock couldn't look dowdy if she tried. Even her scuffed boots were stylish. Her faded jeans fit loose enough to be comfortable but hugged her curves all the same. She'd tucked her wear-softened denim shirt into the waist of her jeans, pulling the material taut over her breasts.

He didn't linger there but his libido took note. She'd piled her copper-colored curls on top of her head, likely to get them out of the way. For some reason that hairstyle got to him more than if she'd left it loose. If she had on makeup, it wasn't obvious. For sure she wasn't wearing lipstick.

Her collie Sam shoved his way into the space between her and the doorjamb, his eyes bright with anticipation.

"You brought treats for Sam."

"I might have."

"Better come in before he knocks you down and licks you to death." Moving back, she grabbed the dog's collar.

"Something smells good." He stepped inside and nudged the door closed with his shoulder.

"I had a hankering for hot chocolate. Figured we could have some while we look over the directions."

"Hot chocolate. What a brainstorm. I can't remember the last time I had some."

"I know, right? I make it for Mav and Zach all the time, but it's not just for kids."

"No, ma'am, sure isn't. Great idea. Where do you want me to put the—"

"Let me take it into the kitchen while you get rid of your coat and feed Sam those treats in your pocket."

"First I need to fetch my toolbox from the truck."

"You can if you want, but I have one."

"I'll get mine anyway. You never know what you might need."

"Suit yourself." Amusement twinkled in her eyes.

She was humoring him. She probably had some fancy-dancy set of tools that would put his to shame, but he was used to his, so he'd bring them in. "Be right back." He handed over the cooler and their arms brushed during the transfer. The brief contact registered. Probably wouldn't have if others had been around.

She turned and started through the arched doorway into the kitchen. "I'd advise you to give Sam one of those treats or he'll try to follow you out the front door."

"Will do." He admired her ass as she walked away. He'd never allowed himself to do that when they were in a crowd.

The house was so still. None of the usual distractions demanded his attention except the cold nose pushing against his hand, openly begging for the dog treats he'd shoved in his coat pocket at the last minute.

He gave Sam one of the bone-shaped biscuits. "One for now, and the other one when I get back. Wait there." He slipped out the door and closed it firmly behind him.

Bringing treats had been an impulse the first time he'd come out here almost two years ago. Jess had told him that Desiree adored her Lassie look-alike, so making a good impression on the dog had seemed like a good idea. Now it was a routine, one he'd almost forgotten in his excitement about an evening alone with her.

When he came back through the door with the toolbox, Sam stood right where he'd left him, tail wagging. Fishing out the second treat, he handed it to the collie, set down the toolbox and took off his coat and hat.

"I see you brought *two* bottles of wine." Desiree called from the kitchen. "Could make for an interesting construction project."

"We don't have to drink 'em." He left the toolbox in the entry and walked through the kitchen doorway, followed by an ever-hopeful Sam. "Mostly I needed to fill the extra space in the cooler so things wouldn't slide around." That was his excuse and he was sticking to it.

"We're opening at least one of them." She'd unloaded the cooler and emptied the jars of soup into a soup pot. "That's my favorite kind and I've been meaning to pick up some more. We polished off my last bottle of it the other night after we finished decorating."

"Then I'm glad I brought two." He'd had them sitting in his wine cabinet for weeks waiting for the playhouse to show up. "You'll have one in reserve."

"Unless we finish that playhouse tonight. Then we might have to open the second one to celebrate." She set the soup pot on the stove. "Soup looks good. Is it Mary's recipe?"

"It is." Had she mentioned his late wife on purpose? Mary and Desiree had been close. Maybe that was another strike against him. Taking an interest would feel disloyal.

"I didn't realize you'd turned into a cook."

"Had to when she got sick. Before that I'd pitch in but she ran the show. Once it was my job, I got into it."

"I envy folks who take to cooking." Pulling two mugs out of a nearby cupboard, she poured their hot chocolate. "I never did. Thankfully Marybeth loves it, and now some members of the next generation do, too, so we're covered." She glanced up. "Whipped cream, marshmallows or neither?"

"Whipped cream, please." He glanced at the small kitchen table where a booklet lay waiting. The directions, no doubt. He picked it up and scanned the first page, which promised that the project would be a breeze. That would be nice.

"Good choice." She grabbed a can out of the fridge and created two expertly peaked dollops. "Take your pick."

"You've done that a time or two." As he laid down the directions and chose one of the mugs, the aroma of cream and chocolate added another sensual hit to his already overheated brain.

"Hot chocolate and whipped cream are fun. It's slicing and dicing I'm not crazy about." She glanced at the collie. "Go lie down. He's not giving you any more treats."

With a doggie sigh, Sam wandered over to a corner of the kitchen and flopped down.

Desiree took a seat at the table and gestured toward the chair catty-corner from her. "If you sit there, it'll be easy to go over the directions together."

Sounded cozy. "Have you read them?"

"Gave 'em a quick scan. Did you play with Lincoln Logs when you were a kid?"

"Who didn't?"

"Me, but I bought them for my kids. The playhouse logs will interlock the same way. It might not be as complicated as I feared."

"That's good news." Careful not to tip the mug, he settled into a kitchen chair. "Thanks for making this."

"My pleasure."

He licked away the tip of the whipped cream so it wouldn't end up on his nose and took a sip. Ahhh. Ambrosia. The next mouthful delivered a combo of cool whipped cream and warm chocolate. "Outstanding." He glanced at Desiree, who was watching him and smiling. "What?"

"You should have hot chocolate more often. It makes your face light up."

"Only if it's this hot chocolate. Best I've ever had." He took another swallow. "You may not enjoy cooking, but you rock hot chocolate."

"That's what my kids say, but they're prejudiced." She picked up her mug. "It's nice to hear it from someone who's totally impartial."

He wasn't even slightly impartial, let alone totally impartial. His taste buds could be heavily influenced by the beautiful redhead sharing the table with him. But if his biased opinion had made her feel good, nothing else mattered. "It's great stuff."

"Thank you." She licked the whipped cream, too, before she drank a little. "Not bad."

"Gonna reveal how you make it?" He swirled the liquid, keeping the chocolate from sinking to the bottom and blending the whipped cream in.

"It's not a secret. Back in the day even the kids knew how to make it."

"It's a McLintock family thing?"

"Guess so."

"Then how come I've never had it?"

"The kids grew up and switched to coffee. I wasn't going to make it just for me. I only recently started again because of the grandkids. I almost brewed a pot of coffee this afternoon but then I changed my mind."

"I'm glad you did. This is a treat. C'mon, Dez. What's the recipe?"

Her eyes took on that gleam, the one he'd told himself to disregard. "I could tell you but then I'd have to kill you."

He laughed. She was teasing him, but she'd done that before. "You'd have to catch me first. I'm faster than I look."

The gleam intensified. "So am I."

"Never mind. I'll just ask your kids."

"They've forgotten."

"How about a free ad for your bookstore in the *Sentinel*?"

Her eyebrows arched. "A bribe, Andy?"

"I'm a desperate man."

She flashed him a saucy smile. "You want this bad, don't you?"

"I do." Hot damn. She gone from teasing to flirting.

"Which means I can use it as leverage."

His heart rate picked up. "For what?"

"Not sure yet." Her eyes sparkled with mischief, and something deeper. "I'll let you know."

He held her gaze, his blood pumping fast. "You do that."

4

Harmless banter. That's all it was, right? Desiree had managed to convince herself the playful discussion about her hot chocolate recipe was simply two friends kidding each other.

Then heat flashed in Andy's blue eyes. Nothing playful about that look. Or the answering tug deep in her core. She'd started the teasing. She'd egged him on. The responsibility was all on her.

Now what? The exchange had been far too delicious and if she didn't watch out, she'd get herself into trouble. She didn't want that, even if the warmth sluicing through her felt good.

She nudged the directions toward him. "You'd better look those over while you sip."

He held her gaze a moment longer before giving her a lazy smile. "Yes, ma'am." He picked up the booklet, pulled his reading glasses out of his shirt pocket and began to study the directions.

Whoa. Had his smile always been that sexy? And his lips so tempting? Surely not. She would have noticed.

Although he'd dipped his head to read the pamphlet, her catty-corner view revealed the remnants of that smile — an upward tilt at the edge of his mouth and a slight dent in his cheek. He'd shaved before coming over. She breathed in a familiar citrus scent.

His yoked shirt looked mighty fresh for this time of day, too. Had he showered and changed clothes? That image stirred her up. She'd never pictured Andy in the shower.

Marybeth's words came back to her. *At least he'd look good naked.* Doggone that woman for putting that notion in her head only hours ago. Shifting in her chair, she reached for her mug of hot chocolate.

Dammit, she was trembling. Any attempt to take a calming drink would risk slopping it down the front of her shirt, the same one she'd put on this morning. Unlike Andy, she hadn't taken a second shower and changed clothes in honor of tonight's encounter. Not that it mattered.

Except he'd clearly thought it might. Had he shaved and showered because he had *ideas*? If so, her teasing had given him a clear indication that he was on the right track. Time to derail that choo-choo train. And she would, right after he finished reading.

Just her luck that watching a man read, especially when he wore cool glasses like Andy's, turned her on. Her younger self had been drawn to brawny physicality. Now she prized thoughtful intelligence. At this moment, Andy epitomized that concept.

He looked up and slid the glasses down the bridge of his nose, giving him a sexy professor vibe. "Do you have a rubber mallet?"

"Do we need one?"

"Yep." He showed her the page. "That's how we're supposed to tap the logs in place. I have one at home but didn't bring it."

Taking a look at the instructions gave her an excuse to lean closer and breathe in his aftershave. Nothing like the scent of freshly shaven male to get her blood pumping. "I missed seeing that, but I have one."

"Good." He went back to reading.

She went back to her covert Andy watching. Clutching her hot chocolate in both hands, she took sips while sneaking peeks at him over the rim of her mug. He'd always been nice to look at. Her brain had acknowledged that a long time ago, but recently her libido had become aware of it, too.

Good genes had gifted him with broad shoulders, a thick head of hair and a strong jaw. Laugh lines complimented his handsome face, although during the dark time after Mary's death, he hadn't laughed much. Jess's return to Wagon Train and Maverick's birth had healed his broken heart.

No question he was appealing as hell, but... not the guy for her. She'd had her share of lovers and they'd all fit a profile — footloose rovers with no interest in marriage — the exact opposite of the man sitting at her kitchen table.

A pillar of the community, Andy's roots ran deep, especially now that his daughter had married a McLintock and gifted him with a granddaughter. Word had it that Maverick had hung the moon.

He finished the last page and took off his glasses. "Did you get a look at what's in the two boxes?"

"Haven't opened them. Didn't need to since the directions were taped to the outside. I figure once we cut into those boxes we're committed to building it there. Rowdy Roost will be off-limits for the little kids until Christmas morning."

"Are Zach and Mav scheduled to come over between now and then?"

"Not anymore. I sent out an alert."

"Then we might as well get started." He tucked his glasses back in his shirt pocket. "Ready to unbox that sucker?"

"I am, but first I need to apologize."

"Oh?"

"I shouldn't have flirted with you."

He gazed at her for a long moment. "Because Beau's dad is coming for a visit?"

She blinked in surprise. "You know about that?"

"Beau mentioned it. He brought Mav in for the annual Christmas lunch with the *Sentinel* staff."

"Well, Steven isn't the reason I shouldn't have flirted with you." Interesting that he'd jumped to that conclusion.

He frowned, apprehension flickering in his blue eyes. "Then what is it?"

"I'm pretty sure you have a crush on me."

His expression relaxed and his frown disappeared. "Yes, I do."

His frank acknowledgment took her aback. "That's flattering, Andy, but—"

"Cards on the table. Are you or are you not attracted to me?"

She took a slow breath and let it out. "I suppose I am, but—"

"That's all I need to know." He polished off his hot chocolate, shoved back his chair and stood. "Let's put that playhouse together."

"Wait." She got up, too, which caused Sam to scramble to his feet. "Down, Sam." She turned to Andy. "It's not that simple."

"The playhouse or us?" He picked up the mug and the directions.

"Us. It's complicated. *I'm* complicated. Even though I'm attracted to you, we wouldn't be a good fit."

"I'm aware you're complicated. That's one of your best qualities. I'm also aware you've had a lot of guys in your life and you haven't stuck with any of them. That makes you a risky proposition."

"Exactly! You'd be nuts to get involved with me. Since I care about you, I should never have flirted with you a while ago."

"Did you enjoy it?"

"That's not the point."

"It's the whole point." Tossing down the directions, he set the mug back on the table. He was on the move. "You had fun. So did I." He stepped closer, invading her space.

Her heart stuttered as she stood her ground and lifted her chin. "It was self-indulgent on my part. I was heedless of the potential consequences."

He smiled. "Then let's even the score." Cupping the back of her head, he kissed her.

She froze, momentarily paralyzed by his bold move. What did he think he was doing? Oh. Ohhhh. Her eyes drifted closed. He tasted of chocolate and whipped cream. And he was good at this. Extremely…mmm…yes… more of—

He lifted his head. "Apologies for my self-indulgence." His voice was like velvet.

He'd never talked to her in that seductive tone, the one he probably used in the bedroom. She was so tempted to drag him in there.

Slowly she opened her eyes and looked up, heart pounding. His intense blue gaze took her breath away, or what was left of it. He'd accomplished a lot in those few seconds. She was shaking, disoriented and ready to rip his clothes off.

His smile reappeared, crinkling the corners of his eyes. "That's the look I was hoping for. Didn't know if I'd ever see it."

There it was again, that soft, caressing voice. Who knew he could sound like that? And be so… kissable? She struggled for breath and sanity. "We can't… this isn't a good…"

"I know. Let go of my shirt and we'll go start on the project."

Breaking eye contact, she glanced down. She had a death grip on the front of his clean white shirt. She unclenched her fingers and smoothed out the wrinkles. Good thing she hadn't crushed the pocket where he'd stowed his glasses. '"Sorry."

He chuckled. "You're welcome to grab my shirt anytime. Or any part of me, for that matter."

"Oh, Andy." She stepped back, filled with remorse. "This was a terrible idea. I shouldn't have agreed to let you come over by yourself. I should have known something like this would happen."

"Are you really that worried about it?"

"Yes! I'm not your type. You're not my type. We could make such a mess and that would affect everything."

"I'm a little confused." He looked more amused than upset. "You're attracted to me. That kiss did it for you. I saw the look in your eyes. But you want to back off because there's a possibility of fallout?"

"Not possibility. Probability."

"And here I thought you were the queen of optimism."

"I am! Just not in this case." She paused to suck in a breath. "You said it yourself. I've had a lot of men in my life and I haven't latched onto a single one. I'm not the marrying kind. You are, though, and—"

"Excuse me for interrupting, but that was a kiss, not a proposal." His lips twitched as if he was trying not to laugh. "I don't even have a condom in my pocket, let alone a ring."

"You wouldn't need a condom." She clapped her hand over her mouth. Where had that revealing comment come from?

His eyes widened and then he grinned. "Desiree McLintock. Have you fantasized having sex with me?"

She had no response other than the heat flooding her cheeks.

"How was I?"

Might as well brave it out. "Great, because it was a fantasy, okay? But real life is a whole other ball of wax."

"Sometimes it's a hell of a lot better."

Now that she'd experienced his panty-dampening kiss, he might know what he was talking about. "Sometimes. But that doesn't mean it's a good idea."

"On that we have a difference of opinion. But we don't have time to debate the subject and we certainly don't have time to test it."

"*Test* it? What are you talking about?"

"If we do decide to have sex, and I'm hoping we do, I suggest conducting it as an experiment."

She stared at him.

"I fully expect we'll be amazing together, but if we're not, we'll shake hands and drink a toast to a good try."

Her slow smile was promising. "You're even crazier than I thought."

"I'll take that as a compliment. Go ahead and open the boxes. I'll get my tools."

5

Andy beat it out of the kitchen and stood in the entryway gulping for air. An *experiment*? Where the hell had that come from? Whatever vein of gold he'd tapped into, he hoped he could access it again.

Desiree had been cocked and loaded, ready to shoot him down. Thanks to an effing brilliant suggestion of an experiment, which had popped into his head out of the blue, she'd given him a sexy smile in return. He was still in the game.

And he was more determined than ever. That kiss... whew. The aftereffects still coursed through his system. A hot kiss hadn't sealed the deal, though, no matter how much he wished it had.

The good news — she wanted him. The bad news — mere lust wouldn't be enough to sway this woman. Not at this stage in her life. But his unexpected approach had bought him some time.

Oh, and another piece of good news. The playhouse construction looked straightforward. Unless they ran into a snag, they should be able to finish it tonight.

Toolbox in hand, he walked back into the empty kitchen. Sam had left, too. A side door gave access to the large dining room and two hallways. The one straight ahead led to the empty bedrooms that had once housed her large brood.

Supposedly that's where her old flame Steven would bunk. Andy would do what he could to foil that plan.

But Steven was a problem for another day. The playhouse — and Desiree — needed his attention. He took the recently constructed hallway to his right. It had been created for access to Rowdy Roost, a combination game room and in-house tavern. It was the perfect spot to build the child-sized log cabin.

It also was the logical place for the big family tree and the celebration on Christmas morning now that the family had nearly doubled in size. But nobody had suggested it. Everyone wanted the traditional setup in the living room, even if they'd be elbow to elbow.

As he approached the swinging barroom doors, the rasp of a box cutter blended with Randy Travis singing *Santa Claus Is Comin' to Town.* She'd put on tunes, but he'd bet they wouldn't be romantic. He gave the doors a push and walked in.

She'd chosen to start with the bigger carton. Close by lay a large tarp currently occupied by Sam, who looked up and thumped his tail on the floor as Andy drew closer.

Desiree hadn't heard him yet. As she ripped through one last seam, the fourth section of cardboard dropped to the floor, revealing the bundled logs and roofing. Damned if they didn't look exactly like the toy ones that came in a metal cannister. Same color notched logs, same green roof sections.

Laying the box cutter on the smaller carton, she stepped back to admire what she'd uncovered, hands on her curvy hips. "What do you think, Sam?"

"He thinks it's very cool. So do I."

She turned around. "It's extremely cool." Her cheeks were flushed with excitement. "Better than I imagined."

"I'm glad." God, she was a beauty. He wanted to wrap her in his arms and carry her off to bed, wherever her room was. He'd never been in there, but he'd find it. Good thing he was holding a toolbox to remind him of his priorities.

"Now that we know it's awesome, we should order those extra logs so she can make it bigger as she grows."

"I agree."

"Beau said it'll go on the front porch to start with."

"Pretty cold out there."

"I got them a heater."

He laughed. "Of course you did."

Her eyes sparkled. "Last Christmas was fun, but it's better when they're older."

"And wiser. That little devil figured out I was Santa at the festival."

"You're kidding!"

"I disguised my voice, but she knew. I could tell by the way she looked me in the eye and grinned."

"Little smarty-pants." Her expression warmed. "Seems like yesterday we were crouched on either side of the bed, Jess squeezing our hands while she pushed that sweet baby into the world."

"Uh-huh." Desiree had been his lifeline that day. "I don't know what Jess and I would have done without you."

She flushed. "Thanks. It was a team effort. I was very grateful you were there." She met his gaze, an affectionate glow in her eyes. Then slowly it changed to something much hotter. Her lips parted.

The space between them sizzled. Even *Grandma Got Run Over by a Reindeer* couldn't douse the flames of anticipation licking through him.

He held his breath, awareness sensitizing every inch of his skin. Was she reliving their kiss? Debating whether to chance another one?

And he was loaded down with the damn toolbox.

"Doggone you, Andy." She said it softly. "It's a good thing you're holding that toolbox."

"Just let me put it—"

"No!" Her laugh was breathless. "Well, eventually you'll have to." She stepped back, way back. "I *really* didn't count on this being a problem. We need to finish the playhouse." Anxiety puckered her brow.

He didn't like seeing that. Didn't want to be the cause of it, either. "We will, Dez. The directions aren't complicated. We've got this."

"How long do you think it'll take?"

"If we push it, we could finish tonight."

"By burning the midnight oil?"

"Maybe. Do you have a window tomorrow if we need it?"

"I do. By some miracle I have nothing going on tomorrow or tomorrow night."

"Then no worries. We have plenty of time."

"Good." She dragged in a breath. "Would you like to set that down, now?"

"Sure. Right next to yours." He strolled over to her rolling tower-o-tools, bright red and at least three times the size of his. "Glad I brought it. We'd have been in deep shit if we only had this red one."

She grinned. "I almost texted you a picture after your call this afternoon. But then I decided it would be more fun not to."

"I kind of expected one like this. It suits you."

"Meaning?"

He glanced at her. "You remind me of that saying *Go big or go home.*"

"Huh." She studied him quietly, hands shoved in the pockets of her jeans. "And how do you feel about that?"

"I think it's sexy as hell."

Her breath hitched. "You don't find me intimidating?" There was that light in her eyes again, the one that made his pulse race.

"Let's face it, you're the reigning queen of this little town, so yeah, I'm a little intimidated." He paused. "But I don't intend to let that stop me."

A response flared in her eyes. "I can see that." She cleared the huskiness from her throat. "But we need to put this topic on the back burner while we work on the playhouse."

"Yes, ma'am."

"I admit I'm part of the problem. I didn't anticipate that I'd have trouble controlling... well, anyway... I haven't helped the situation. I'll put a lid on it if you will."

"Absolutely." Short-term sacrifice for long-term gain. As a younger man, he'd had trouble with that concept. These days, it was a piece of cake. "Let's do this."

6

What a novel situation. Desiree chuckled to herself at the joke. Although she was usually adept at handling a mutual attraction, she'd seriously underestimated the strength of this one. Andy Hartmann was damn near irresistible.

But she hadn't become Desiree McLintock, aka bestselling author M. R. Morrison, without learning how to focus.

She gestured to the large canvas tarp on the floor. "I figured we'd build the playhouse on that so we can drag it over to the door when it's time to load it."

"Looks like we'll be building it around Sam."

"He'd love that, but he'll be on his bed, which I brought in because I knew he'd like to supervise. But I'll let him have the tarp for now."

"Have you measured Beau's truck bed to make sure it'll fit?"

"We're not using it. We're renting a flatbed to take the sleigh into town on Christmas Eve, so might as well transport the playhouse on it, too."

"Good thinking. I keep meaning to ask how you made out with the sleigh ride tickets. I saw Joe

Wilson in the hardware store the other day and he and his family are so grateful for this fundraiser."

"We sold more than enough. Since Angie and Kendall are donating their time, it'll just be materials. Soon that family's kitchen will be operational again."

"I'm impressed Cheyenne got them to admit they were in financial trouble."

"He's always on the lookout. After any structural fire, he follows up on his own time."

"Did he dream up the sleigh ride idea?"

"We all did. We'd planned to take the sleigh to town again this year since last year was such a hoot. Selling tickets to benefit this family was a no-brainer. Did you buy one?"

"I bought quite a few. Gave away all but two, which are in the last time slot." He held her gaze. "Want to take a sleigh ride with me on Christmas Eve?"

What a romantic gesture. The roomy sleigh could hold more than two. If he'd saved five tickets and chosen an earlier time, they could have included Beau, Jess and Mav. He hadn't done that. Her silly heart thumped faster. "Yes, I would."

"Great." He smiled. "It'll be fun."

Well, shoot. She had the urge to kiss him again. Sucking in a quick breath, she cleared the lust from her brain. "Might as well go through the contents of the big box first, make sure it's all here."

"It will be."

"What makes you so sure? Usually they leave out at least—"

"I know, but this is a special project for a special little girl."

"Those are the ones that are guaranteed to have missing parts."

"Wait and see. This time will be different." He flashed her a grin. "Trust me."

Oh, hell. He might as well have said *kiss me*. Why did he have to be so adorable? "Evidently I'm working with a cockeyed optimist."

"Takes one to know one. Do you want to unpack or read the list?"

"I'll read. You unpack."

"Okay." He handed her the instructions.

She looked at them and squinted. "Hang on. I need to get my glasses."

"Try mine." He pulled them out of his shirt pocket. "They're just readers."

"That's all I use." She slid them on and glanced at the print. "That works. Thanks."

"Very nice."

She glanced up. Oh, no. A sexy gleam was back in his eyes and her body responded. "Stop looking at me like that."

"Can't help it. I've never seen you wearing cheaters."

His use of the word tickled her. He had an extensive vocabulary and knew how to use it. "I don't unless I'm reading or writ— working on the computer." Whoops. This encounter had become so personal she'd momentarily forgotten he wasn't privy to her secret.

"Seems strange that I've never been around when you're doing those things."

He wasn't supposed to see her doing those things. She'd been careful about that. She offered a handy excuse. "We're always in social settings. The first time I saw you wearing yours was this afternoon at my kitchen table."

"Clearly it didn't turn you on."

It had, but she'd keep that info to herself. "You're turned on by seeing me in glasses?"

"Weird, I suppose. The cliché is true, at least for me. It makes people look smarter. I've always been attracted to brainy women. I already know you're extremely intelligent. Adding glasses is icing on the arousal cake."

She snorted. "The *arousal* cake? Where did that gonzo expression come from?"

"I just made it up. But you get the idea."

Oh, she got the idea, and it was becoming more persistent with every minute they spent in each other's company. "Enough about glasses and subjects we've decided to table."

"Yeah, sorry about that. I'm on it." He walked over to the stacked pieces of the log cabin and began pulling off each bundle, calling out the contents and arranging everything alongside the tarp.

Nothing was missing.

He gave her a triumphant smile. "See?"

"So far, so good. Moving on to the small box." She turned to the next page of the instructions.

"Gotcha." He picked it up and set it on the top of her red toolbox.

He had her, all right. She'd told Marybeth that sex with Andy wouldn't be happening. Now it was all she could think about.

When he opened the carton, she pictured him undressing her. He would be good at that, too, his fingers gentle, capable, caressing....

"Dez? You getting this? I'm not hearing you say *check*."

"Sorry." She scrambled to find her place on the list of parts. "Could you repeat that last thing?"

"Twenty three-inch washers?"

"Um, no." She'd missed the first three things on the list. "Better take it from the top."

"Yes, ma'am." He gave her a quick glance, that tempting mouth curved in amusement. He was onto her.

They made it to the bottom of the box. Miraculously every part on the list was accounted for.

Andy looked please with himself. "Told you."

"I'm shocked. All these parts and they didn't miss a one. This company's got it goin' on. If the playhouse goes together easily, I'm writing a review online."

"I'm sure they'd appreciate it." He surveyed the array. "Might as well get started."

"Are you hungry?"

"Depends on how you mean the question."

"Andy...."

"Awww, I couldn't resist. If you think about it, this setup is hilarious. We've known each other for twenty-seven years and yet we've never been alone."

"That can't be right."

"Why would we? No reason for it. We wouldn't be alone tonight if I hadn't specifically requested it. I'm glad I did. I could have gone on for months blissfully unaware you're hot for my body."

She laughed. "Not me. I already knew you were hot for mine."

"I'm not surprised. I'm a heart-on-my-sleeve kind of guy." He paused. "I have a thought."

"I'm sure you have several."

"I do and I'm saving them for later. What if we start building and see how far we get in an hour? Then we'll break for dinner. At that point we'll have a fair idea of how long the rest will take."

"I like it. I could turn the stove on low so the soup can be slowly heating while we work."

"Great."

"I'll be right back." She handed him the instructions. "Just in case you want to get a jump on it."

"I just might. I'm motivated." He gave her another one of his winning smiles.

She hurried out through the swinging doors, lit up by the sensual wattage of that smile. The guy had so many arrows in his quiver. She hadn't factored in his quirky sense of humor or his ability to use the language, or his audacity.

He was bolder, braver, and more inventive than she'd ever given him credit for. If anyone had asked her yesterday if she knew Andy, she would have claimed to be well acquainted with his virtues and foibles. And she would have been wrong.

She'd learned more about him in less than an hour than she had in their months of interaction. He fascinated her. That still didn't guarantee a good time in bed, though.

Flipping on a light in the kitchen, she turned on the heat under the soup and gave it a few stirs with a long wooden spoon. Even cold it smelled delicious. One more facet of him she hadn't known.

Being wooed by Andy was thrilling so far, but she'd be wise to keep her feet firmly planted on the ground. This flirtation was unlike any in her past.

She'd become accustomed to life as a single woman and had no wish to change her setup. Her instincts told her Andy might take up more space than she was willing to surrender.

Armed with that insight, she left the kitchen and headed down the hall to Rowdy Roost. Alvin and the Chipmunks were warbling away, which made her giggle. She'd loaded the sound system with a bunch of silly holiday tunes to squelch any chance of funny business. So much for that plan.

She pushed through the swinging doors and paused. Sam lay in the bed she'd brought in for him. Andy knelt on the tarp, his sleeves rolled back to his elbows, his attention focused on the logs he'd lined up for the foundation.

The sight of his muscular forearms shouldn't affect her. She was aware he kept himself fit. Several times this summer she'd seen him in a T-shirt.

But a barbeque with the family couldn't compare with this intimate setting he'd engineered. A glimpse of his bare skin created an intimate tug of longing made stronger by the knowledge that he wanted her.

At least he'd look good naked.

Moisture pooled in her mouth. Curiosity was a valuable gift in her work, a potential snare in her personal life. Was he a good lover? Only one way to find out. If he wasn't, then she'd take him at his word, shake hands and toast a good try.

But what if he was?

Z

When Desiree called time, the project was about where Andy had figured it would be — a little less than a third complete. The logs were tight, which was a good thing. The rubber mallet was their go-to tool.

If they'd had two of them, the work would have gone faster. They'd taken turns swinging it and he'd come to respect the force she brought to the task. Although she had plenty of help running this ranch, she likely could do any of the required jobs if necessary.

He sat back on his heels and looked over at her. She'd taken charge of the back and one side wall. He'd handled the front and other side wall. "Not bad for an hour's work."

"Not bad at all. I'd like to say we only have a couple hours left, but in the next phase we'll be putting in the windows and that'll be trickier."

"Much trickier. Looks good, though. Sturdy."

"Built to last, they said. I asked Bret and Molly if Zach would want something like this and they said he was more into kid-sized vehicles, so that's what I got him. But I predict he'll pester his folks to take him to her house more often once this is in place."

"You're giving him the kiddie car on Christmas morning?"

"Yessir."

"I just realized we'll have two toddlers, two four-month-old babies and a newborn. If we're lucky at least the newborn will sleep through it, but—"

"Are you suggesting it'll be a zoo?"

"That's what I'm saying."

"It will be. And that's just how I like it."

Her wide smile sent a rush of warmth through his chest. He couldn't help smiling, too. "Evidently, or you wouldn't have raised so many kids. I don't know how you managed that."

"I had Buck and Marybeth."

"Even adding them, you were still outnumbered."

"But not outsmarted."

"Now that I believe." Earlier she'd returned his glasses, but he'd hung onto the image of her wearing them. Another side of a multi-faceted woman.

She rose to her feet. "Let's go have some of your soup and open a bottle of that wine. Come on, Sam. Dinnertime."

The collie pranced along beside her, toenails clicking on the wood floor.

Andy followed Sam with a similar level of eagerness in his step. Dinner sounded good. His stomach rumbled. He could use the mellowing effect of a glass of wine, too.

Working closely with Desiree for a solid hour while staying focused on the job had been a challenge and he'd met it, by God. That didn't mean he wasn't wound a little tighter than he would prefer.

Rather than work in silence, he'd chosen the safest topic on the planet — their grandchildren. Although he was only biologically entitled to claim Mav, he'd happily agreed to be the honorary grandpa for the others, starting with Zach after Bret married Molly. Zach had the Grandy nickname down pat.

Serving that function for Kendall and Cheyenne's little girl Jodie had been a given since Kendall had lost both parents. Then it had seemed logical to include Sky and Penny's little girl Susie, who'd been born twelve days after Jodie. Zach's baby sister Elvira had arrived on Thanksgiving, bringing the number to five in less than two years.

And as Desiree often reminded him, this was only the beginning. He'd enjoyed the role immensely, especially because it brought him closer to her. That said, he'd never celebrated a Christmas involving that many little kids. It would be an adventure.

"I'll feed Sam first." Desiree walked into the fragrant kitchen and opened the oversized fridge. "If you remember where the soup bowls are, you're welcome to dish that up."

"I remember." He knew his way around every room in the house except one — the critical one at this point. Not only hadn't he been inside her bedroom, he had no clue where the door was.

While Desiree scooped dog food into Sam's dish, he took out bowls and plates to set them on. "Are we eating in here?"

"That would be more efficient."

He balked at efficiency. It was their first meal with just the two of them. "Why don't I make us a small fire? We could turn on the tree lights and eat in there."

She let out a soft sigh "You know, that sounds lovely. If you want to go make a fire, I'll dish the soup and slice the bread."

That sigh arrowed straight into his heart. She was a dynamo but reason told him she had to get weary now and then. He'd talked her out of asking Beau and Jess to help with this project, at least doubling the load on her.

He hadn't factored that in, had he? A little late in the day to change things. Beau and Jess would be enjoying their evening, probably in front of their own fireplace while reading Mav a story before tucking her in bed.

After switching on the tree's multicolored lights, he moved the fireplace screen and opened the flue. He pulled the smaller lengths of split wood from the wrought iron holder Bret and Gil had made from used horseshoes. He had a small blaze going when she came in with two wineglasses and an open bottle.

He stood. "I'm a jerk, Dez."

Her eyes widened. "Where did that come from?"

"I was so intent on spending time alone with you that I saddled you with extra work. If we had Beau and Jess helping, you wouldn't have nearly the—"

"Hold your horses, cowboy." She handed him a wineglass. "You're making some big assumptions." She poured him a full glass and did the same for herself. "Have you heard me complaining?" She turned and set the bottle on a small table flanking the sofa.

"No, but I heard that sigh when I suggested eating by the fire. Sounded like someone who's been pushing herself. And I've added to your workload."

"First of all, you haven't added much. You brought dinner so I didn't have to think about it. If they'd come, I would have made a meal for all of us, hauled out the highchair and put fresh sheets on the crib. Although I love Mav to pieces, she does take effort."

"But we might have finished the playhouse tonight. I doubt we will on our own."

"Then we'll finish it tomorrow." She touched her glass to his. "Here's to our first unchaperoned meal." Lifting the glass, she held his gaze while she sipped.

He followed her lead, keeping eye contact while taking a swallow and praying he wouldn't choke on it. The way his pulse was racing, he could easily ruin this moment.

She wasn't irritated with this setup. Instead the warmth in her eyes reflected gratitude. She lowered the glass. "It's been a long time since I relaxed in front of the fire with..." Her mouth curved. "A man who had the hots for me."

Yeah, he liked the direction of this conversation. Liked it a lot. "I'm sure plenty would have volunteered, me included."

"I've had a few offers, but for one reason or another, I sidestepped them. Decided maybe I was over all that."

"Seriously?"

"The last time I went out with a guy, he spent the evening giving me a detailed description of his colonoscopy."

He grinned. "Did he bring pictures?"

"It was a first date, for crying out loud!"

"How many dates before I can discuss mine? I'd hate to do it prematurely, but on the other hand, I'm sure you're gonna want to hear about—"

"Stop." She swatted his arm.

"That's why you gave up dating? Colonoscopy guy? Maybe you just needed to shoot for someone a little younger."

"I got that advice. Both the Wenches and my kids said so, but it doesn't appeal to me. I'd rather be with someone who listened to the same music I did when I was a teenager, who remembers how we used to dress, the movies we watched."

"I get that." And it was very good news. "But one bad apple shouldn't—"

"There were two. The guy I was seeing prior to the colonoscopy dude was a decent conversationalist. We had lots in common. But when we started getting friendly, it turned out he was wearing a spandex thingamajig to flatten his tummy."

"No."

"Can I assume from your shocked expression that you're not wearing spandex?"

"I'm not, but if you'd like me to prove it, I'll be glad to—"

"Don't take off your clothes."

"Ever?"

"I didn't say that." She gave him a sassy once-over. "Just not now, please. Let's enjoy the fire, the Christmas tree and the meal you've provided."

"Yes, ma'am." He set his glass down next to the wine bottle. "Why don't you have a seat on the sofa and enjoy your wine? Your waiter will arrive shortly with your dinner."

"Don't you dare come back shirtless."

"Not my style. I don't remove my shirt until it's time."

She laughed. "Time for what?"

"I think you'll figure it out." He waited until he was in the kitchen before allowing himself a fist pump. Bless his faithful old weight bench. He'd had it for years, had often thought of abandoning his routine.

Looked like he'd be stepping it up.

8

Taking Andy's suggestion, Desiree sank onto the sofa, nudged off her boots and propped her sock feet on the edge of the round wooden table. What a treat, especially with the sparkly tree nearby, its pine scent mingling with the richness of burning cedar.

She sipped her wine and basked in the heat from the fire. Great move on Andy's part. She hardly ever built one out here just for herself.

The fireplace was massive, suited to the large room and the generously sized furniture. She'd been going for the Ponderosa look from *Bonanza*, and by golly, she'd achieved it.

She'd collected sturdy pieces that could be reupholstered as needed — a sofa, two loveseats and various easy chairs. The sofa and matching loveseats formed a U-shape facing the hearth. The table in the middle stood knee-high, tall enough for drinks and snacks, board games or even a simple dinner. Good for propping up her feet, too.

When the whole gang arrived on Christmas morning, she'd open up the space and add easy chairs to the semi-circle as needed. Dining chairs might come into play. In a pinch, pillows on the floor worked, too.

In the early days she'd often slept out here on cold winter nights with Sky, Beau and the twins. Her heating system had burned oil and she couldn't always afford a delivery. They'd pretended to be cowpokes on the trail. Fun times.

"Dinner is served, milady." Andy's bootheels clicked on the wide-plank floor. "Watch out for the soup. It's very hot."

Putting down her wineglass, she glanced over her shoulder.

He walked toward her looking exceedingly pleased with himself. No telling where he'd found that big ol' tray. Steam and a mouthwatering aroma rose from the soup bowls.

Happiness bubbled in her chest. "This is starting to feel like a party."

"Because it is." He rounded the loveseat on her left and deposited the tray on the table. "One that's been a long time coming."

She leaned forward and pulled the tray closer. "Are you saying this night was inevitable?"

"Maybe." He turned his head to check on the fire. "Let me goose that up a little."

"Not too much. We still have to—"

"Been thinking about that." Moving the screen, he chose two logs slightly larger than the ones crackling on the grate and tucked them gently into the blaze. After adding new fuel, he watched to make sure the logs caught before replacing the screen.

She appreciated a guy who took the time to do it right. A valuable trait for... many things. "Do you like building fires?"

"Oh, yeah." He came around the table and picked up his wine glass and the bottle on his way. "It's a new experience every time, even when you know the fireplace well. I haven't had much experience with this one, but I'm getting a sense of how to work with it."

"That was the first thing I put money into. The windows leaked, the door didn't shut properly and the roof was on its last legs. I ignored all that and hired a mason to build me a big rock fireplace."

He nodded. "I would have done the same. It's the heart of the house."

"Well said." She picked up her glass. "To warm hearts."

He tapped his against hers. "To warm hearts." Then he laughed as Sam appeared and laid his head on his knee. "And cold noses. Someone followed me."

"I see that. He probably needs to go out."

"I took him out after he finished his dinner."

"You did?" This guy was handy to have around. "Thank you so much. Okay, Sam. You've been fed and taken out. Go lie d— oh, wait. I left your bed in Rowdy Roost. That's why you're bugging us."

"I'll get it." Andy put down his glass.

"But then we'll just have to haul it back out there again."

"Not necessarily." He met her gaze. "Here's my thought. The work would go twice as fast with another rubber mallet. Why not postpone construction until I bring mine tomorrow? It's a more efficient use of our time."

She grinned. "Why do I get the idea there's more than efficiency on your mind?"

He returned her smile. "Am I wrong about the mallet?"

Now she was tingling all over and some places more than others. "You're not wrong."

"I'll get Sam's bed."

Had she just agreed to something that would land her in trouble? Quite likely. "I'll top off our wine."

"Yes, please." He stood. "Come on, pup, you gotta move so I can get out." Coaxing Sam to back up, he headed toward the dining room, the collie glued to his side.

"I'll bet you gave him another treat while you were in the kitchen together."

"Or maybe he's just fond of me."

She chuckled. "I'm sure that's it." She took time to appreciate the view of the fit of his jeans and his loose-hipped stride until he and Sam disappeared down the hallway to Rowdy Roost.

Then she added a little wine to their glasses and transferred the soup bowls, breadbasket, utensils and napkins to the table. Soup was a good choice for this setup. Less awkward than plates.

Had he anticipated they might eat by the fire? Or hoped for that? It was the most romantic spot to share a meal other than her bedroom and romance had been on his agenda, so maybe.

When he'd first arrived, his solo presence in her house had struck her as exotic and unsettling. But the longer he was here, the more she relaxed and allowed herself to enjoy the experience.

Might as well face it, being alone with him gave her a buzz and she'd missed that feeling. Even better, the sexy vibe developing between them came naturally, without fanfare, as if they were settling into a familiar groove.

But that was impossible. They had no groove to settle into. As he'd pointed out, they'd never spent time alone. He'd had to work to make it happen. This night hadn't been inevitable, even if the word kept popping into her head.

Why was that? Oh. Because she wanted it to be a foregone conclusion. That let her off the hook. If sex between them was bound to happen, no matter what, she didn't have to take responsibility for any fallout. *Not your style, girlfriend.*

By the time he returned with Sam's bed, she was clear on that point. The decision to get horizontal wasn't written in the stars. She had complete control of this evening.

Instead of asking her where to put the dog bed, he set it down in the exact right place — near the hearth but far enough away to avoid stray sparks.

"You've been paying attention."

"It's what I do." He gave the fire another glance before coming back to sit beside her on the sofa. "When I was a kid I was either going to be a detective or a reporter. Then I figured out a reporter was part detective so I went with that."

Spreading his napkin in his lap, he picked up his soup bowl and dipped his spoon into it.

She followed suit. "Not much detective work in a small town like Wagon Train."

"Oh, you'd be surprised."

She glanced at him. Something in the way he'd said that… nah, she was being paranoid. But it brought up another issue. If she agreed to this *test* he'd mentioned, she'd have to tell him her secret.

She'd been debating doing it anyway. She'd held off, though. He'd claimed her standing in the community didn't intimidate him much, but that was the tip of the iceberg,

He'd written glowing reviews of her work, calling her *the most talented voice in Western literature today*. He was a fan in a way that none of her other partners had been.

"Hey, Dez." His voice had taken on that velvet quality again. "Something bothering you?"

She blinked and shook her head. "No. Your detective remark had me picturing you wearing a Sherlock Holmes hat and smoking a pipe."

"Sorry. Didn't mean to derail the program."

"No worries. Gave the soup a chance to cool off a bit." She quickly took a spoonful and hummed with pleasure.

"Like it?"

She nodded, finished chewing and swallowed. "Excellent." Scooping up some more, she savored the rich flavor. She hadn't tasted Mary's in years, but she'd swear this was better.

Andy paused between mouthfuls. "I had a Sherlock Holmes costume for Halloween when I was eight."

"And where were you then?"

"Indiana. Went to Purdue, then got a job at the Journal & Courier, which is where I met Mary. We'd only been married a couple of years when we heard a weekly was for sale in Montana."

"And you could afford it?"

"No. My folks cosigned the loan or we'd never have been approved." He handed her the breadbasket. "You need some of this."

"I do. Thanks." The bread was sliced thick, just the way she liked it.

"Dip it in the soup. It's really good that way."

She dunked it partway, took a bite and reveled in the moist yumminess. Fun with food. Andy kept making points. She continued the dipping routine until she polished off the slice. "Awesome."

He chuckled. "Want another one?"

"Yes, please."

He handed her the breadbasket again. "How about you? I know you moved here from Apple Grove. Were you born there?"

"Yep. Had no idea who my dad was. I don't think my mom did, either. She was young, flighty, not particularly motherly."

"That's too bad."

"It wasn't optimal, but she gave me the freedom to do whatever I wanted, and she was a good example of what I didn't want. I got a job, saved money and got my own place when I was seventeen."

"Hm."

"This bread and soup combo is outstanding." She popped the last bite of her second slice into her mouth.

"I'm glad it's a hit." He put down his empty soup bowl, picked up the wine bottle and emptied it into their glasses. "What happened to her?"

"I don't know. Two years after I moved out, she announced she was leaving town with her newest boyfriend. I never heard from her again."

"Ouch."

"I know it sounds like she abandoned me."

"Because she did abandon you."

"But what if that was for the best?" She spooned up the last of her soup from the bowl. "I was more mature at nineteen than she was at thirty-seven. It might be a blessing that I was spared seeing how her life turned out."

"Maybe so."

"You know what they say." She set her empty bowl on the table and picked up her wine. "Whatever happened in your past got you to where you are. If you're happy now, then why wish for a different past?"

He took a sip of his wine. "And are you happy now?"

"Very much so. I have a wonderful family, terrific friends, a lovely place to live, good health, fulfilling work. What more could I want?"

He glanced at her. "Is that a rhetorical question?"

"It is." She smiled. "And let me say it's a pleasure to have a discussion with a man who uses the word *rhetorical*."

"And let me say I was hoping it was a real question and you wanted me to give you an answer."

Her pulse quickened. "Do you have an answer?"

"Yes, ma'am."

"Let me guess. You think I need a sex life."

"I wasn't going to say that."

"Then what?"

He drained the last of his wine and set it down before turning to her and resting his arm on the back of the sofa. "I was going to say you're a lucky woman to have all those things and better yet, you know it."

"Oh, I absolutely do. I'm grateful." She clutched her wine glass, hesitant to take a drink. A shiver of anticipation traveled up her spine. The intensity of his gaze told her he had more on his mind.

"I took a chance when I kissed you. You could have thrown me out on my ear." He paused. "But you didn't."

She resisted pressing a hand to her chest. Her heart was beating *so* fast. "No."

"Based on your response, I'm thinking you're not quite ready to give up *all that*, as you put it."

She put down her wine before she spilled it. Then she mimicked his posture, shifting to face him. This was it. Decision time. "In other words, I need a sex life."

"Uh-uh. You need way more than a sex life. You need a lover. And I'm officially applying for the position."

9

Desiree's soft gasp and the heat that flared in her hazel eyes sent shock waves through his system. She wanted to say yes, but would she? Had his direct approach been brilliant or a colossal blunder?

"You have cojones, Andy."

"I have a hunch that you admire that, but I could be wrong. The meal's over except what's left of the wine, and we have a plan for tomorrow. If I just ticked you off, feel free to send me home."

Her breathing sped up. "The meal's not over. I promised you Christmas cookies."

"I'd ten times rather have a kiss than a Christmas cookie."

"You haven't tasted these cookies. They're primo."

"But I've tasted you and no cookie could compete. You're delicious."

Color bloomed in her cheeks. She cleared her throat. "That thing you said before, about treating it like an experiment — were you serious?"

"Yes, ma'am. If we give this a shot, we need to promise each other we'll tell it like it is after we're done. The unvarnished truth. That's mostly on you since guys are notoriously easy to please."

"You mean while we're still lying there, I'm supposed to give you a thumbs up or thumbs down?"

"Better than hemming and hawing around. Say it quick, get it over with, never have to talk about it again."

"I thought we were going to drink a toast to a good try."

"You have a good memory."

"Like an elephant."

"Okay, so we get dressed, pour two stiff drinks — whiskey would be my preference — and toast each other. We'll toss back those shots and then I'll leave."

"Like a gunslinger after a bar fight?"

"Something like that. It has more class than me scrambling out of bed and leaving like my tail's on fire."

"But you want me to give you my review while we're still in bed?"

"The sooner the better. After you catch your breath. I'm assuming you'll be breathing hard. If not, then—"

"I don't think I can give you that review. I mean certainly I can if it's thumbs up, but after you've knocked yourself out, I couldn't just—"

"You're right. You're too kind to give it to me straight and that's perfectly okay. Never mind. I'll know without you telling me, unless you're really good at faking it."

"I've never faked an orgasm in my life."

He blinked. "Never?"

"Why on earth would I? The thought never occurred to me. When Charley told me some women do that, I was—"

"Charley? Sky's dad?"

"Yes, and I apologize. I have a rule never to mention a former partner when I'm with...." Her breath hitched.

"Your current one?" His chest tightened. "Does that mean a yes? Or a no?"

"Neither. It's an exceedingly conditional, completely revocable, subject to extensive examination... maybe."

"Damn, woman. Have you memorized the dictionary?"

She gave him a little smile. "I like words."

"That's like Leonardo da Vinci saying he likes paint, but we're veering off topic. How can I convince you to give me a chance?"

She stared at him. "Why would you compare me to Leonardo da Vinci?"

"It's not such a stretch." He gazed at her and sighed. Might as well get this out of the way. "You're a helluva writer, Dez. I wasn't sure when we'd stumble onto that subject, but—"

"You know who I am?"

"I do, and I figured we'd get around to that sometime tonight. I guess now's the—"

"Since *when*?"

"The bookstore was a major clue, but I began to suspect years before that, after Mary had been in your book club for a while."

"You discussed it with her?"

"Oh, hell, no. I would never have put her on the spot. If I was right, and the Wenches were your beta readers, then logically she'd been sworn to secrecy, just like everyone in your family. My hat's off to all of you. Well done."

"I'm speechless. No wonder your reviews have been so—"

"Hey, hey, don't even go there. I write rave reviews because you deserve every word of them. I was impressed by M. R. Morrison from the get-go, before I knew it was you. Every book is better than the last. You—"

"I can't believe you haven't said something before now."

"As noted previously, we've never been alone."

"You could have found an opportunity!"

"When? Certainly not when Mary was alive. It would have thrown you into a panic and upset Mary, who'd think she'd somehow given it away. I wasn't about to show off my detective skills at yours and Mary's expense."

She regarded him quietly for a long moment. "That says a lot about you. You could have put the *Sentinel* and Wagon Train on the map."

"And betrayed a friend. Not even slightly worth it. I don't believe in cutthroat journalism. That's why a small-town weekly that relies on local features is where I belong."

"But it's still a newspaper, and after my career took off, this would have been newsworthy. I wasn't expecting that level of success when I asked Mary to be on the team. But I worried about it later. I knew she'd be careful, but I did worry about you."

"Because you didn't know me."

"That's for sure." She rolled her eyes. "I was convinced I'd successfully flown under your radar."

"I was fine with that."

"What did you think two years ago when Jess wanted to write a feature about why my kids all have iconic Western names?"

"I tried to talk her out of it, but I had to back off. I was afraid she'd get suspicious that *I* was hiding something."

"And aren't we glad she did that interview?"

"Tell me about it. Maybe she would have ended up with Beau eventually, but there's no guarantee."

Desiree let out a gusty sigh. "Thank you, Andy. You've been a faithful steward of my secret. Sorry for coming unglued."

"You're welcome, and that's perfectly okay. I didn't mean for it to come out quite like that. But now you know I'm capable of discretion, which could come in handy."

She went on alert. "I'm not sure what you mean."

"You're on the fence about me, which I totally understand. We have a very nice arrangement as it stands. You're afraid we'll screw it up."

"Yep."

"But as we've proven, we're experts at keeping our mouths shut. And that's how we'll contain any fallout from this new endeavor. We can't screw up anything if we don't involve the kids."

"But they're already involved, unless you didn't ask Jess if they'd help with the playhouse."

"Actually I did. I told you I would so I felt obligated to mention it to her."

"And then what? You took back the request?"

"More or less."

"Does she know why?"

"Yes."

"Then she'll tell Beau."

"I'm sure she will."

"And the speculation will spread through the family from there. How can you say the kids won't be involved?"

"Because we simply won't talk about it. If they ask questions, we'll just smile and say *no comment.*"

"They're not stupid. They'll have a pretty good idea if something's going on."

"So what? We'll neither confirm nor deny. For all they know we spend our time together playing gin rummy."

"Would you like that?" She threw him a teasing glance. "I can fetch a deck of cards."

"I don't want a deck of cards." He slid his hand under the collar of her shirt and cupped the back of her neck. So warm. "I don't want sugar cookies." He leaned closer, heart thudding in his chest, his body taut. "I want you."

She swallowed, the soft sound heading straight to his groin. A *yes* glittered in her eyes, but he needed the words from her sweet lips.

He was tempted to kiss her again. She looked as if she expected that. But a make out session on her sofa wasn't what he had in mind. They weren't kids anymore.

Massaging the tight muscles in her neck, he held her gaze. "Now it's your turn. The meal's over. The fire's burned down to embers. What do you want, Dez?"

<u>10</u>

Andy was giving her the choice and she appreciated that. Although she was within kissing range, he held back, respecting her right to make a conscious decision. But he continued that slow, sensual massage of her neck.

She struggled to marshal her thoughts when his touch made her ache in a way she'd assumed was gone for good. He was sexier, smarter and more principled than any man she'd known since Charley. Her body pulsed with demands that would soon wipe out her common sense.

"I have…" She had to stop and clear her throat. "I have some conditions."

The heat in his eyes intensified. "Name 'em."

"You need to leave before anybody else is up. No staying for breakfast."

"Wasn't planning to. If the kids find me at your kitchen table, might as well announce it on the front-page of the *Sentinel*."

"Also, if we continue to see each other you should probably come and go through the back entrance to my bedroom."

"I thought the back door went into the kids' wing."

"There's another one on my side of the house. It's almost invisible. The kids know about it and sometimes the Wenches use it. But they all respect my privacy and don't monitor whether anyone's parked back there after dark."

He smiled. "Clandestine. Kind of appeals to me."

"It does? I thought you'd hate it."

"I don't hate anything if it means I get to share your bed." He held her gaze. "Anything else?"

"One more. Marriage." The word came out a tad breathlessly.

"I thought you'd never ask."

"Smartass. I just want to make it clear that I'm—"

"Not the marrying kind? I get it. You won't see me dropping to one knee unless my old football injury acts up."

"You played football?"

"Yes."

"What position did—"

"I think someone's stalling." He kissed her, his mouth claiming hers with practiced ease. Cupping her head in both hands, he held her firmly in place while he created chaos in her quivering body.

Game over. With a moan of surrender, she wound her arms around his neck and crawled into his lap.

A low chuckle rumbled in his chest. He lifted his mouth. "That's what I'm talkin' about." And he returned to the kiss, taking it deeper, stroking his hands down her back and gripping her tush with strong fingers.

Mmm. Getting hot on this sofa. Should move, but when his mouth... was so... nice....

He pulled back, gasping. "I'd carry you off to bed, but..." He gulped for air. "I don't know where—"

"Come with me." Scrambling off his lap, she put both feet on the floor, grabbed his hand and tugged.

He stood so quickly she almost lost her balance. Sam popped up, too, tail wagging.

She gave the command automatically. "Lie down, Sam."

"Does he sleep in your room?"

"Yes, but—"

"Let him come in. We'll tone it down."

She blinked in astonishment. At this point in the action, no man had ever given a second thought to the dog in her life.

"Sam adores you. So far he likes me, too. I don't want him to see me as the guy who steals you away for hours every night."

"*Every* night?"

"Every night you'll have me."

"I don't think I'm ready for—"

"One night at a time, Dez. One night at a time."

She soaked up the combination of amusement and desire in his gaze. Despite his own needs, he'd considered Sam's. After all these years, she was going to bed with a grownup.

Taking his hand, she led him toward the library with Sam trotting close behind.

"Oh, my God." He started to laugh. "You sleep in the library. I should have known. Is there a Murphy bed in the wall?"

"I do not sleep in the library."

"Then I'm confused. There's only one door... wait... a revolving bookcase?"

"Brilliant deduction, Sherlock." Releasing his hand, she rounded the circle of wingback chairs the Wenches used for meetings. A slight nudge to the bookcase on the far wall set it in motion.

"This is very cool, Dez. I can't wait to see your—oh." The panel glided smoothly on its track, gradually revealing her large office and a Christmas tree in the corner. "It's not your bedroom." He walked in, his glance sweeping the room. "It's where the magic happens."

"Not all of it." She held his gaze as she slowly undid the top button on her shirt. "I save some for the next room."

His chest heaved. "I just bet you have."

His admiration for her work combined with his lusty interest in her was a heady combination. She added a gentle sway to her hips as she approached the double doors where Sam stood waiting to get in.

After tidying up her bedroom this afternoon, she'd closed the doors because opening them for a visitor created a more dramatic effect. She'd cleared the clutter in her office, too. Without admitting it to herself, she'd visualized exactly how the evening would go.

She gave Sam a hand signal to stay back before she opened the double doors.

The lights from her Christmas tree cast the room in a soft romantic glow and drawn curtains heightened the intimate mood. She'd arranged logs in the beehive fireplace and draped a holiday throw over the armchair sitting nearby.

No doubt about it. She'd pictured Andy standing on this spot and she'd wanted to impress him. Evidently she had.

"Wow." He paused. "Feels like I should take off my boots."

"Take off whatever you want, cowboy." She undid another button, pulling his attention away from the room.

His hungry gaze took in the cleavage exposed by her partially unbuttoned shirt before lifting, searing her with the heat smoldering in his eyes. His voice was husky. "I thought I knew what I was in for." He sucked in a breath. "I underestimated."

"Gonna change your mind?"

"Hell, no." He toed off his boots. "I'll just recalibrate."

"Then come on in." She walked through the doorway. Once Andy was in, she beckoned to Sam, who trotted straight to his bed and plopped down with a big doggie sigh.

Meanwhile Andy's focus had switched to her king-sized bed. "I doubt that came from a department store."

"A woodworker in Missoula made it."

"To your specs?"

"Yes. Clint was a teenager and this project inspired him to get into woodworking."

"I can see why. It certainly inspires me, but along different lines." He crossed the room and brushed his fingers over the smooth log at the foot of the bed. Three larger ones made up the headboard.

He gripped one of the corner posts and she experienced a visceral tug in her core. Connecting rails at the top created a canopy frame that she'd left undraped to highlight the beauty of the honey-colored wood. Those polished logs made for a sexy bed. Tonight she was more aware of it than ever.

She'd bought a new comforter a few months ago — a forest, mountain and valley print on a cream background. She loved it, and when Andy ran a hand over the soft cotton, she trembled, eager for his caress.

He turned back to her. "Your bedroom is beautiful, Dez. I'm honored that you let me into... well, it's your sanctuary, isn't it?"

"Yes." He understood that this place was special, private, available by invitation only. She closed the distance between them and slid her arms around his neck. "I'm glad you pushed for this. I'm glad you're here."

He pulled her close. "I'm so glad I'm ready to jump out of my skin."

"How about jumping out of your clothes, instead?"

"Time to check for Spandex?"

"Definitely." Heart pumping fast, she reached for a button on his shirt. "You might want to find out if I'm wearing any."

"Be glad to." He gently pulled her shirt from the waistband of her jeans, laid his palms against the small of her back and stroked upward, pausing to unhook her bra with practiced ease. "So far, so good." Leaning back, he gazed into her eyes, slid his hands past her ribs and cupped her breasts. "No spandex." His voice was ragged with tension.

She held her breath, her unbuttoning forgotten. "That feels... so good."

"I can't believe—" He cleared his throat. "I'd better not wake up and find out—"

"It's real." Taking hold of her shirt, she pulled it over her head, scattering hairpins everywhere. Then she dispensed with her bra and stood before him, her breasts quivering, her hair arrangement destroyed. "I'm real."

He sucked in a breath. "Magnificently real."

"And *hot*. You get me so hot, Andy."

"Message received." He scooped her into his arms.

"Hey! Don't hurt yourself!"

"Shush. It's three steps to the bed." He laid her on the comforter and had her out of her jeans, panties and socks in no time.

She lay there gasping. "But you're still dressed."

"Ladies first." He unbuttoned his shirt partway and pulled it over his head the way she had. Dropping it to the floor, he gestured to his lightly furred chest. "No spandex."

"I can see that." Marybeth was right. He looked good naked, at least the top half. He hadn't developed those pecs writing op-eds for the *Sentinel*, though. "You work out."

"So do you." He unbuckled his belt. "Where's your equipment?"

"In Lucky's room." Tossing excess pillows to the floor on the other side, she kept her eye on him as she shoved the comforter, blanket and top sheet to the foot of the bed. "His old set. When he moved out, he...."

She lost track of the conversation as Andy kicked away his jeans and shoved down his knit briefs. Regular workouts could improve and sculpt his body, but certain attributes depended entirely on genetics. He'd been genetically blessed.

"You're staring, Dez."

"So did you, Andy. And to borrow your phrase, you're magnificent. Bring that lovely package over here, please."

He climbed in beside her. "It's not what you've got, it's what you do with it." He rolled to his side, facing her.

"Something tells me you'll do just fine." She stroked his chest, her fingertips dancing over his springy chest hair. She started to reach lower.

"Not yet." He caught her wrist. "It's been longer for me than for you."

She met his gaze. "Not by much."

"You didn't go to bed with Spandex guy?" He let go of her wrist.

"I pretended to get an urgent text from Marybeth about the ranch so I could beat it out of there."

"You were at his place?"

"Of course. I wasn't going to bring him *here.*"

"But you brought me here."

She cupped his face in both hands. Smooth cheeks. Smart man, to shave just in case. "No comparison. I've always known you were special. Ever since Mav was born, I've known I'd eventually tell you about M. R. Morrison. But I was never going to tell him."

     "Not even if you had sex with him?"

     "That's just my body. My work is my soul."

11

Just when Andy had begun to get his bearings, Desiree had stunned him with another revelation. Allowing him into her creative world was more meaningful to her than inviting him into her bed.

He should have guessed that, but he hadn't. Maybe because he was a man, he'd put more importance on the physical connection. Or maybe it was because his balls ached as if he'd hit them with a sledgehammer.

"So you see," she continued, her palms warm against his face. "Even if this experiment doesn't work out for us, we'll still be thick as thieves. You're part of my inner circle, now."

Sliding an arm around her waist, he tugged her closer, mostly so she didn't have enough room to grab hold of him. He might not survive even one gentle squeeze. "I was in the know before. You just didn't realize it."

"And the fact you didn't say anything is huge. That puts you in a whole other category."

"I take it that's a good category?"

"Very good."

"Maybe I should quit while I'm ahead."

"Don't you dare."

"Just kidding. Roll over, pretty lady. Let's get this party started." Giving her an orgasm before the main event would ensure he wouldn't completely blow the program.

"Happy to." She stretched out on her back. "Climb aboard, cowboy."

He followed her over. Propping himself on his forearms and his knees, he gazed at her lying beneath him, rosy and inviting. The soft glow from the Christmas tree nearby highlighted every delicious detail. He dipped his head and brushed his mouth over hers.

She murmured something.

"Hmm?" He lifted his head.

"Let's skip foreplay." She rubbed his back.

"Meaning...."

Her breath quickened. "I don't need preliminaries. I'm juicier than I've ever been in my life. I want you. All of you. Please."

A surge of pure lust shook him to his toes. "We'll be headed for premature city, no side trips."

"What if we call this a practice run?"

"Huh?"

"You know, a warm-up."

"It'll be more like a flame-out." But God, he was tempted. His control was slipping fast.

"So we'll get that one out of the way. It won't count."

"You won't have time to come. Let me—"

"Yes, I will." She slid her hands lower and pressed her fingers into his glutes. "Please, Andy. You know you want to."

He clenched his jaw. "You have no idea."

"Then do it." Her grip tightened and she lifted her hips.

His breath hissed through his teeth. She'd put herself in the perfect position. He could feel her heat. He eased closer. The tip of his cock made contact. Looking into her eyes, he drove deep.

She moaned and pushed upward. So lush, so hot. By some miracle, he didn't come. But he would soon. The pressure was intense. With a sharp inhale, he drew back and rocked forward. The potent friction made his ears buzz.

"More."

Her eager plea summoned his inner twenty-five-year-old. It was the only explanation. How else was he able to thrust into her over and over without coming?

She quickly caught his rhythm and urged him on with breathless cries. Any second his climax would end this insane run, but until it did, he'd abandon himself to the incredible pleasure of loving Desiree the way she was supposed to be loved.

Then he felt it, a brief undulation. He stroked faster. There. Another, and another, getting stronger. Panting, she called his name, arched her back, and shivered against him as she bathed his cock with a rush of moisture.

Gasping, he plunged deep one more time and let go, spilling into her, his rhythmic response blending with hers, his body shuddering. Gulping back a shout of joy, he gazed into eyes shining with happiness. Victory.

Her lips curved in a lazy smile. "Not bad for a practice run. Were you sandbagging me?"

He took a shaky breath. "No, ma'am. I surprised myself."

"Nice surprise."

"I had more control than I expected. Not sure where it came from, but I'm grateful."

"When we first walked in, you said the bed inspired you. Maybe that was it."

"More likely it was you." Leaning down, he kissed her, taking his time, relaxing into the afterglow of good lovemaking.

She kissed him back, clearly enjoying the process. Slackening her jaw to give him access, she gripped his head, shoving her fingers through his sweat-dampened hair.

When she began sucking on his tongue, his cock twitched. Probably an aftershock. Their connection was still snug, another fascinating development. Shifting his weight to his left arm, he cradled her breast and stroked his thumb over her nipple.

It grew tight as a freshly picked raspberry, making him hungry to taste her. At her earlier request he'd skipped that treat and it was one he particularly enjoyed. He slowly ended the kiss. "I feel the urge to nibble."

"Be my guest."

His bad boy responded to her low murmur with another twitch. "I figured I'd better ask." He stroked her silken skin. "Technically it's foreplay."

Her sexy chuckle made her breast quiver under his palm. "More like after-play."

He grinned. "So foreplay's out but after-play works for you?"

"Sure does. Especially when we're still extremely well connected."

He couldn't explain why that continued to be true, but he'd take it. Cupping her breast, he leaned down and drew her pert nipple into his mouth, rolling it over his tongue and paying attention to her breathing. It picked up.

So did his. Massaging, nibbling and licking, he coaxed a moan from her sweet mouth. She was sensitive here, which suited him just fine. He would have been sad if she hadn't much cared for this part.

When he began to suck, she gasped. His cock got a gentle squeeze. He doubled down, hollowing his cheeks, taking more. The next squeeze signaled she was ready for action. And saints be praised, so was he. This was one for the record books.

She dragged in a breath. "Andy."

Gradually ending his caress, he nuzzled his way back to her mouth and dropped a soft kiss there before lifting his head to look into her eyes. They sparkled with a mixture of desire and laughter. "Yes, ma'am?"

"We have...." She gulped. "A situation." Wrapping her arms around him, she lifted her hips, increasing the depth of their connection. "I'd like you to do something about it."

"Yes, ma'am." Holding her gaze, he eased back and slid forward, creating a slow, steady pace. "Is this what you had in mind?"

"Uh-huh. This is... unexpected."

"I know." He watched her eyes darken as he continued to stroke. "But I like it."

"Me, too." Her breath hitched. "Come closer." She pressed down on his back.

He lowered his chest until he was almost touching her breasts. "Like that?"

"More. I want to feel you..."

Sinking down, he brushed across her taut nipples as he rocked back and forth. "Like that?"

"Yeeesss." Color bloomed in her cheeks and she sucked in a breath. "So good..." She began to pant. "So... good..." Her muscles clenched and with one sharp gasp she came, her channel rippling as her soft cries blended with the liquid rhythm of his thrusts.

He rode the crest of her orgasm, prolonging the pleasure until his release shouldered its way forward and took over. With a hoarse cry, he surrendered to a climax that hit him with the power of a tsunami. Shock wave after shock wave left him gulping for air. Resting his forehead on her shoulder, he gave her some of his weight as he fought to keep from collapsing onto the woman of his dreams.

"Easy, cowboy."

Her murmured words penetrated the ragged sound of his breathing. "That was... epic."

She let out a happy sigh. "Sure was." She cupped the back of his head, massaging gently. "I could get used to this."

His heart stuttered. Slowly he lifted his head. "Is that so?"

The corners of her mouth tilted up. "You're a lot of fun, Andy."

Sounded like she wanted to keep it light. He was good with that. "So are you, Dez. Do we have a deal?"

"I believe we do."

"Hot damn."

12

Desiree gazed up at Andy, still giggling inside. Did he realize how far he'd blown past her expectations? Probably not. He was a humble guy.

Maybe this gig was a mistake and she'd live to regret inviting him into her bed, but... c'mon. He was an amazing lover. And great to look at. And funny.

Leaning down, he kissed her on the tip of her nose. "I hate to move, but I think it's time I relocated."

"What, you're not going for a third round?"

"Just so you know, I have no idea how I managed a second round. I doubt it will ever happen again. If that's your reason for greenlighting this endeavor, then—"

"It's not, although your staying power was impressive."

"Thank you. I'll admit it was. How do you feel about cuddling after sex?"

"I like it."

"Good." He eased away from her. "So do I."

"How do you feel about a jacuzzi after sex?"

He blinked. Then he glanced toward the bathroom door and chuckled. "I should have guessed."

"We don't have to. Cuddling works. I just thought maybe—"

"Are you kidding? What idiot wouldn't want to indulge in a private jacuzzi with a beautiful woman?" Swinging his legs over the side of the bed, he stood and turned to hold out his hand. "Let's go."

"Awesome." She let him help her out of bed. "It's not everyone's cup of tea."

"Clearly not Sam's." He tipped his head toward the dog bed. "He hasn't stirred."

"He probably won't. You were right to suggest bringing him in with us. Now that he knows I'm safe with you, he can relax."

"That's what I was hoping for. Get him used to seeing me here by myself." He gestured toward the bathroom. "Shall we?"

"Stay here a minute. I need to set the scene." Hurrying into the spacious bathroom, she used the glow of the nightlight as she turned on the water and touched a match to her array of candles in frosted glass holders. "Okay," she called out, turning off the nightlight. "Come on in."

He appeared in the doorway looking rumpled and sexy. Joy fizzed through her veins. She wouldn't want to send him home when the time came. She would, though, because keeping this development under wraps was a good plan.

He came toward her. "You dazzle me, lady."

"I like putting that look on your face, like you just got exactly what you wanted for Christmas."

"I did." He pulled her close. "I even got it two days early."

"I thought I didn't need a Christmas present this year, but I was so wrong." Savoring the press of his body against hers, she brushed her fingers lazily over his chest. "You outdid my fantasy, by the way."

"No kidding? How?"

"So many ways. You're such a good kisser. I mean really outstanding. I didn't guess you'd be so well endowed, either, and I'd never seen you shirtless. I didn't know you'd have lovely chest hair." She reached up and touched his cheek. "You're blushing."

"I can't recall ever standing naked while a woman catalogued my attributes."

"Well, you asked."

"You're right, I did. It's a habit, asking questions. But since I opened that can of worms, I'll ask another one. What's so great about chest hair?"

"I find it extremely sexy. But I didn't think about it the first time. I was in a big hurry. I just wanted the basics."

He grinned. "The basics, huh? Good thing I didn't fold after that or I'd have been toast."

"No, you wouldn't. After that first round, you had me. But the next time, when the pace was slower, I remembered your chest hair." She scrubbed her fingers over his pecs. "Feeling you brush back and forth over my skin drives me wild."

"Lucky me." His reply was husky, as if this topic was getting him hot.

Wouldn't bother her a bit. "Lucky *me.*" She glanced over at the jacuzzi. "It's full enough." Moving away from him, she turned off the water and switched on the jets. "Ready?"

"Getting there."

The way he said it made her look over her shoulder. Sure enough, he was rising to the occasion. "You're a miracle of nature, Andy."

"I still say it's you."

"If so, I'm flattered." As warm water swirled and bubbled, she stepped over the lip of the tub onto the bench seat. "Mm, temperature's just right." She sat down and slid over to give him room.

Climbing in, he settled next to her. His breath hitched. "That's unique."

"Which part?"

"Bubbles dancing around my privates. I've been in a jacuzzi before, but not naked."

"Does the sensation bother you?"

"No, ma'am. Turns me on, though." He leaned back.

"Not a bad thing, right?"

"Not considering I'm in here with you. Is that why you like this? It gives you a buzz?"

"One of the reasons. But as I was reminded tonight, a jacuzzi can't take the place of a good lover."

"Nothing takes the place of a good lover." He let out a sigh. "I told myself I was getting along just fine, especially after Jess moved back and started working with me at the *Sentinel.* For about six months I was perfectly content. I had everything I needed."

"That's about the time I came to the same conclusion and gave up on dating."

"Then Jess told me about the baby."

"Icing on the cake."

"That's how I saw it. Time to switch gears and embrace my role as a doting grandfather."

"My exact thought when Beau told me."

He gazed at her breasts, only partly covered by the churning water. "I don't think the grandfather role suits you, Dez."

She snorted. "You know what I mean."

"Yeah." He reached for her hand under the water and threaded his fingers through hers. "Grandparents don't have sex. Everyone knows that."

She laughed. "It's unseemly."

He gazed at her, a gleam in his eyes. "When did you start fantasizing about having sex with me?"

"After we went through Mav's birth together."

"Bingo." He squeezed her hand. "For me, too."

"Those are the moments that stir up basic instincts."

"Yup."

"All that emotion, and tension, and I'll admit it, some fear."

"Oh, yeah. I've had scary moments with Jess, but nothing to compare with that."

"But you hung in. The way you coaxed Jess through it stirred me up."

"I kept glancing over at you, with your hair coming undone and your breasts heaving, and that light in your eyes. When it was all over, I wanted to haul you out in the woods and have my way with you."

"I would have gone if you'd asked me."

"Damn it. That's what I get for being a coward."

"But you finally got around to making your play."

"Took me fourteen effing months, though." He sighed again. "I was convinced you didn't think of me that way or you would have taken the initiative. I'd make a fool of myself by letting you know how I felt, and you'd say no, thank you."

"I was prepared to say that. Until you kissed me."

"I'm not sure I would have without the hot chocolate conversation. Which reminds me, do I get that recipe or not?"

She laughed. "I can give you the recipe, but wouldn't you rather come over here and have me make it for you? It won't be the same if you make it for yourself and sit there drinking it alone."

"Tell me about it."

"I loved the way you licked the whipped cream before you took a sip."

"I loved the way you watched me over the top of your mug."

"You saw me doing that?"

"You keep forgetting — observing is my superpower." He turned to her. "Are we gonna have sex in this jacuzzi?"

"Would you like to?"

"I would, but I'd rather not drown in the process."

"I won't let that happen."

"Good, because finding me eating breakfast in your kitchen would be nothing compared to finding me drowned in your jacuzzi."

She snickered. "You have a dark sense of humor. I've never seen that side of you."

"I'm a man of many parts."

"And I'm a woman of many parts. Sit right where you are, and I'll see if I can fit two of those parts together. How does that sound?"

"Like you've never done this before. How long have you had this jacuzzi?"

"It was a Christmas present to myself two years ago."

"Uh-huh. What do you say we move this project to dry land?"

"Aw, c'mon, Andy." She let go of his hand and stood. "Don't you want to cross jacuzzi sex off your bucket list?"

"Is it on yours?"

"It is, now." She positioned herself in front of him. "Just pretend you're sitting on the side of the bed."

"With flood waters swirling around me. Got it."

She gripped his damp shoulders. "You're a little slippery."

"If you think my shoulders are slippery, wait'll you get to the rest of me."

"That's what I want to find out." She braced a knee on either side of his hips. "What it feels like when our significant parts are submerged."

"Wet. Very wet."

"In other words, super lubricated." She dropped her voice to a soft purr. "Won't that be exciting?"

"Maybe." He spread his hands over her tush and his breathing changed. "You could be onto something."

"I could be onto *you* if you'll help me. Guide me in. I'll go slow to start with." She held her breath as he positioned her. When his cock nudged the perfect spot, she tightened her grip on his shoulders. "Let me set the pace."

His gaze locked with hers. He nodded.

Sliding down added movement to already moving water. The stimulation factor was insane.

Andy's low, intense *ahhhh* made her laugh. "Told you!" Clutching his shoulders as best she could, she began to move — slowly at first since she'd promised, but then faster.

He didn't complain. He did cuss, and that made her laugh even more. Then she had no more breath for laughing because she was coming and coming hard. So was he. With one earthy, appropriate swear word, he shoved upward, locking himself in tight as he shook and swore some more.

She leaned her forehead against his and held on until the waves, both internal and external, subsided. They'd sloshed a bunch of water on the floor. She didn't care.

Releasing his hold on her backside, Andy lifted his dripping hands out of the water, cradled her head and tipped it so he could give her a long and lingering kiss. Then he pulled back. "I'll never doubt you again."

She smiled. "Thanks for going along with it."

"Lesson learned. Go along or miss out. And when it comes to you, I don't want to miss a thing."

13

Andy worked side-by-side with Desiree mopping up the bathroom floor. Their jacuzzi adventure had been spectacular, a cymbal crash that would make a perfect ending to the evening.

Instead of crawling back into bed with her, which he longed to do, he would leave. This wasn't a relationship to sink into. It was one to navigate.

He wrung out the towel he'd been using, searched for a spot to hang it, and ended up using the glass-block wall of her walk-in shower. "Nice shower. Roomy."

"Big enough for two, although neither of us needs a shower right now."

"That's for sure."

She ran her fingers through her damp hair. "So much for glamor."

"You're beautiful and I hope you know it." He reached for her, allowing himself one more moment of holding her close.

"Thank you. I was lucky to have a beautiful mother. I take after her."

"Do you have pictures?"

"A couple. Tucked away. Because of her, I learned not to put importance on my looks. She capitalized on hers, finding guys who would support her, at least until they figured out they were just a bank account."

"What about her parents? Did you have contact with them?"

"They disowned her when she got pregnant with me. I suspect that kind of nastiness and neglect was a recurring cycle. I was determined to break the chain and create a life that made me happy and my kids happy."

"And now you've made me happy." He could stare into her hazel eyes for hours. Always something new to see there — the heat of passion, the twinkle of amusement, the spark of an idea. "Saying thank you seems lame, but... thank you."

"You're so welcome."

"It's time for me to go home."

"Go home?" She frowned. "The sun won't be up for hours."

"I don't want to stay until then, much as I'm tempted to cuddle with you in that amazing bed."

"Why don't you want to stay?"

"Because we'll fall asleep, and I'll have to set an alarm to make sure I get out of here on time before Sky shows up at the barn."

"If it's the alarm you hate, I have this wonderful soft chime, with a light that gradually brightens. It's way better than a typical alarm."

He made a mental note of that for later, when he was more secure in this arrangement. "It's not the alarm. It's leaving you. Doing it now is a whole lot easier than forcing myself out of your warm bed and into a cold December morning."

"Good point. In your shoes, I wouldn't like that, either." She hugged him and let go. "I'll help you collect your clothes. Maybe next time we won't feel the need to throw things on the floor."

"Speak for yourself." He pulled on his briefs. "Tonight was one hell of an icebreaker. I'll be more eager, not less."

She handed him his shirt. "So will I. I don't know what I was thinking. I'll want you naked immediately."

He thanked her for the shirt and put it on, which wasn't nearly as much fun as taking it off. "How do you see things working out tomorrow? Should I come in through the front in the morning and through the back at night?"

"Let me think about that." She went over to a door. A light came on when she opened it, revealing a custom walk-in closet, likely built by the same guy who'd created the revolving bookcase. Her wardrobe was extensive and bursting with color.

He looked away and continued dressing. His journalist's instincts wanted to know every personal detail about her. He'd have to tie and gag those instincts and wait for her to give him info whenever she cared to.

She came out wearing a plush royal purple bathrobe. His breath caught. Even with wet, disheveled hair, she looked like a queen.

"It's tough to let you go home when you stare at me as if you want to do it all again. And again."

He swallowed. She held all the cards. If she dropped the robe, came over and kissed him, he'd stay. "I do want that." He cleared his throat. "But it's best if I take off."

"Then I'll walk you to the door."

He nodded and followed her out of the room. The click of doggie toenails on the wood floor told him Sam had decided to join the goodbye party.

He cast a longing glance at her office on the way through. What he wouldn't give to browse through her research materials.

"You can prowl around in there tonight if you want."

He laughed as they made their way through the library. "I dunno. If the choice is between exploring your office or exploring you, your office comes in a distant second."

"So here's a thought." She walked out of the library and turned back to him. "What if I tell the gang that I let you in on the M. R. Morrison thing and I found out you'd known for years?"

"Fine with me." He glanced down at Sam, who stood beside him, tail waving. "You good with it, Sam?"

The collie's tongue lolled out and he wagged his tail harder.

He laughed. "Sam's onboard."

"He would be. He likes everyone to be on the same page. So do I, really. This will be a relief. We can all relax on Christmas Day. Last year you were the only one here who didn't know, or so we thought."

"I picked up on that. And I had to pretend I was clueless. I considered announcing that I knew, but the potential for blowing up my first McLintock Christmas stopped me from uncloaking."

"Then it's a plan. I'll start with Jess first thing in the morning, before I blast it out to everyone. I don't want her to think for a moment that she or her mom gave it away."

"Thanks. Better it come from you than me."

"Also, if everyone's focused on that subject, it might distract them from speculating on what we're up to."

"Or make it worse, but I don't care. Getting M. R. Morrison out in the open is worth it." He grinned. "As soon as everyone knows, I'll be free to go into your office during the day and *prowl around*." He made air quotes.

"Not much to see."

Uh-oh. Was that a flash of anxiety in her eyes? "Dez, I won't overstep. Your office is part of your sanctuary and I get that. I'd want you to come with me, show me stuff."

The tightness in her expression disappeared. "I have an uncirculated copy of *Hondo*."

"No kidding? I figured you might be into Louis L'Amour."

"You have no idea." She gave him a saucy look. "But I believe you said you were leaving."

"I don't want to. A sexy lady writer with a taste for Louis L'Amour is almost impossible to resist." He paused, took a breath. "I'm going." He headed for the entry.

She and Sam followed him over. "I admire your self-discipline."

"I'm telling myself I'll be here most of the day tomorrow." He grabbed his coat and shrugged into it. "We'll talk while we build the playhouse."

"Of course we will. And when I call Jess, I'll tell her the playhouse may take us the rest of the day to complete."

"Which it might." Especially if they took a break so she could show him around her office.

"After the horses are fed and Sky's gone home, it'll be dark and you can move your truck around back." She pulled an electronic key fob out of her pocket. "This opens the door to my bedroom."

As he took the key to her bedroom and all the pleasures that it promised, his body tightened, making it hard to concentrate on specifics. But she hadn't said anything about food. "What about dinner? Want me to—"

"We'll finish up the soup and I'll make toasted cheese sandwiches. We'll eat in front the beehive fireplace."

"This is sounding better and better. But it reminds me I left you with supper dishes."

She waved a hand. "No worries. That'll take me five minutes. You need to get out of here before you change your mind."

"I do." He plucked his hat from the coat tree. "Do you think we can pull this off without the kids being the wiser?"

"Maybe not, but if they sense we don't want to be open about what's happening and we need space to figure things out, they'll leave us alone."

He nodded. "You're right. They're respectful."

"There are only two people I plan to tell."

"Marybeth and Buck?"

"Marybeth is one. She's like an older sister to me. She comes and goes whenever she wants."

"Good to know."

"That doesn't include my office or my bedroom, though. Nobody's allowed in those two rooms without an invitation. Anyway, it's better if she knows. She won't give us away and neither will Buck if she tells him."

"Then who's the second person?"

"Steven."

"Ah." He probably looked smug. It took willpower to keep from grinning. "Because of me. Now he can't stay here."

"No, you're the reason he *can* stay here."

"What?"

"I'd really hate for Beau and Jess to put themselves and Mav through the trouble of making a place for him. Maybe eventually they'll add on and it would be fine, but now it's a royal pain."

"But won't it be a royal pain for you if he's here?"

"Not if he knows I'm involved with you."

"Oh." That was some consolation. The info would keep the guy in one of those twin beds on the other side of the house during the night, but during the day....

"Judging from little hints he dropped during our conversation, he's sick of the constant traveling. Since I'm still conveniently single, if he manages to reignite the flame, he can settle down here."

Not on his watch, damn it. Better not say that out loud. "You don't sound enthusiastic about the idea."

"It *horrifies* me."

Hallelujah! He ducked his head to cover his reaction.

"Okay, that was a little harsh. I'll always be grateful for our time together. He gave me Beau. But after his visit last year, I realized what we had is over. I can't imagine a fling, let alone a long-term relationship with him."

Emotions under control, he looked up. "I understand. Things change."

"The fact is, I can't imagine a long-term relationship with anyone." Her gaze was steady. "You've said you get that, but—"

"I absolutely do. We're on the same page." He'd interrupted her, but he couldn't say it fast enough. If he ever triggered her marriage phobia, he'd be gone. "What's funny is that Steven's bid to stay with you is what built a fire under me."

She smiled. "I wondered about that."

"I'd dithered around for months and I finally had an opening. No way was Steven effing Jacobson gonna short-stop me."

"Oh, Andy." She giggled. "He wouldn't have. But I'm glad you thought he might."

"Me, too." He pulled her close. "Listen, if you want me to have a talk with him, set him straight, I'll be glad to."

"I'll bet you would. I wish every grandma could experience the thrill of two grandpas fighting over her."

"It's not a fight. I've already won."

"True." She pulled his head down and gave him a quick kiss. "Now leave before I lose my resolve and seduce you."

"You could, you know."

"Of course I could. Get out of here, Hartmann."

He put on his hat and touched two fingers to the brim. "So long, Dez. See you bright and early." He opened the front door.

"Don't forget the rubber mallet!" she called after him.

"Yes, ma'am! On my list!" Damn, it was arctic out here. Made his cheeks hurt when he grinned. But he couldn't control the big ol' smile on his face. Maybe she wouldn't have given Steven another turn at bat, but thanks to him, Grandpa #2 was benched.

_14_

Desiree woke up with a smile on her face, picked up the phone on her bedside table and glanced at the time. She'd slept in, and she never slept in. She hadn't conked out like that in years.

Coffee. The familiar aroma meant Marybeth was here. She sat up, checked Sam's bed. Empty. Marybeth had fed him. That's why he hadn't pestered her to get up and she'd enjoyed a whole extra hour of shuteye.

See you bright and early. She bounded out of bed. Exactly what qualified as _bright and early_?

Grabbing her purple robe off the foot of the bed, she put it on and tied the belt. She'd slept nude for the first time in ages. She blamed Andy for that decision.

When she pulled on the drapery cord, sunlight slapped her in the face. Made her laugh. Definitely _bright_ out there, but she'd blown the _early_ part to smithereens.

As she padded barefoot through her office and into the library, Marybeth's voice drifted from the kitchen. Either she was on the phone or—

A familiar warm baritone replied. Andy. She ran her fingers through her hair. It had dried while she'd tidied up last night and she'd brushed it before going to bed, but maybe she should head back and grab a hair tie.

Oh, what the hell. She planned to confide in Marybeth anyway and the sound of Andy's voice made her eager to lay eyes on him. Just then he chuckled over something Marybeth had said. Her heart lifted and her step quickened.

Because she was barefoot, they probably hadn't heard her coming. Slowing her approach, she paused just outside the kitchen door, struck by the normalcy of the scene.

They stood talking about Mav, each with a mug of coffee in hand, perfectly at ease as if they'd established this routine years ago. Fascinating.

Andy had on a pair of faded jeans and a flannel shirt in red buffalo plaid that begged to be touched. He looked taller next to Marybeth, but so did everyone in the family except Zach and Mav.

Desiree cleared her throat. "Good morning."

They turned in unison, each wearing smiles of welcome. Marybeth's eyes twinkled.

Andy's held a more intense glow. "Good morning, sleepyhead."

His affectionate tone made her skin tingle and her cheeks heat. If Marybeth hadn't guessed the status, she knew it now. "Sam usually gets me up." She glanced at her dog curled in the corner, head on his paws, clearly unfazed by this new person hanging around.

Marybeth lifted her mug. "Coffee?"

"Love some."

Andy drained his. "You'll need a bite to eat, too. Any objections if I go in and get started?"

"No objections, but I won't be long. I'll just grab something quick, throw on my clothes and be there before you know it."

"Take your time. I showed Marybeth what we have so far and she thinks we'll finish today, no problem."

"Oh, yeah." Marybeth nodded. "Now that you'll each have a rubber mallet it'll go twice as fast." Her voice quivered as if she wanted to laugh but was holding back. He must have told her the mallets were the reason they'd stopped working. Clearly she wasn't buying it.

At least he'd remembered to bring another one to back up the story. "If we'll easily finish today, why not stay and have another cup of coffee while I eat breakfast? We have cinnamon rolls in the fridge. We can warm up a couple."

"That sounds tempting, but I'm itching to get back to it." Rinsing out his mug, he put it in the dishwasher. "Unless you don't want me to—"

"That's fine. I'll get there as soon as I can."

"No rush." He held her gaze. "Promise me you won't gobble down your breakfast."

"I promise."

"See you in a bit." And off he went.

She stared after him. "He turned down a cinnamon roll. Who turns down one of my famous cinnamon rolls?"

"A man who is eager for you to give me the four-one-one so he doesn't have to edit every word that comes out of his mouth." Marybeth poured coffee into a mug and handed it over.

"Was he doing that? He looked so relaxed."

"Granted he was amazingly calm, considering what must have been going through his mind. The man has poise. And layers."

"He does." Desiree took a sip and put down her mug. "I'll just scramble some eggs." She pulled a frying pan out of the cupboard.

"Let me scramble the eggs. You talk."

"I can scramble and talk."

Marybeth rolled her eyes.

"It was just the one time."

"And that particular frying pan has never recovered. I know you're gonna tell me or you wouldn't have arrived in your bathrobe. Make the toast, please." She got out the eggs and cracked three into a bowl.

"How do you know I won't have a cinnamon roll?"

"Because when you're sleeping with a guy, you get worried about love handles."

"I'm having a cinnamon roll. Want one?"

"You *didn't* go to bed with him last night?"

"Oh, I went to bed with him and it was fab-u-lous. Life-affirming. Fun as hell." She pulled a container from the fridge, took out two cinnamon rolls and put them in the toaster oven. "I'm warming you a cinnamon roll, too, by the way."

"Sure. Thanks." Marybeth whisked the eggs and dumped them in the pan. "Must be something different about Andy."

"There's a lot that's different about Andy. He's been through some stuff and obviously he's been strengthened by it. He's self-aware but not selfish. He stopped me from locking Sam out of the bedroom last night. That's when I realized I'm dealing with an honest-to-God adult."

"What a pleasant surprise. Does that explain the cinnamon roll?"

"Yep. He knows me. He gets me. I can be myself and he's fine with that. In fact, the real me is the attraction."

"That explains why you waltzed in here without doing your hair and makeup."

"And did you see the way he looked at me?"

"I did. Figured if I hadn't been here, he would have greeted you... differently." She grinned.

"Um, yes." Transferring the warm cinnamon rolls to small plates, she set them on the table and paused to listen. The faint tap, tap, tap of a rubber mallet gave her goosebumps.

"Got your eggs." Marybeth put a fork on the plate of fluffy scrambled eggs and handed it to her. "Go ahead and start. I'll bring us more coffee."

"Thank you. I take it Andy had already eaten?"

"He had. Looked well rested, too, which I found curious. So do you."

"Because he didn't stay late. We'd planned he'd leave before sunup and that way he'd miss Sky driving in. But he decided it would be harder to leave if he stayed, fell asleep and then had to drag himself out of here."

Marybeth nodded. "Good thinking. So now what?"

Between bites, she outlined the strategy for keeping the relationship on the downlow. "I don't expect drama, but if there is, I don't want the kids to be part of it."

"Andy's part of the family. They're bound to be somewhat involved."

"To some extent. They'll be aware something's going on, but we won't be hugging and kissing in front of them."

Marybeth gazed at her in silence for a long moment.

"What? Spit it out."

"First of all, I'm thrilled about this. I've felt the connection growing between you guys ever since the day Mav was born. It's just... he's in love with you."

"I know. I'm a little bit in love with him, too." She paused. "You're worried he'll want a commitment I'm not willing to give."

"Yes, ma'am."

"We've already talked about it. He's not looking for that with me."

"What is he looking for? Besides the obvious."

She gave herself a moment. "I'm thinking... romance. That's what I'm looking for, and he might be, too. He likes the clandestine part of coming to my back door after dark. That's a clue."

"Like I said, he has layers."

"And here's another one. He figured out that I'm M. R. Morrison years ago."

Marybeth froze, the cinnamon roll halfway to her mouth. "How?"

"Just put clues together. He used to think he wanted to be a private detective."

"Did he tell Mary?"

"Nope. He thought if he told her, she'd blame herself for inadvertently giving it away. Which she hadn't. He came to the conclusion on his own. Then he sat on it until last night."

"Damn. Now I'm really impressed with the guy."

"I am telling the kids about that. I'll call Jess today, so I can assure her that she and her mom had nothing to do with him finding out. Then I'll spread the word."

"That'll make Christmas easier. No dancing around the subject anymore."

"And maybe that revelation will throw the kids off the trail."

Marybeth laughed. "Have you met these kids?"

"Yeah, you're right. They'll be curious as hell. But if we don't give them fodder for gossip...."

"Hang on. I see something." Marybeth stood and peered out the kitchen window. "Don't look now, but you're already in trouble. Sky's coming across the yard headed for the porch."

She leaped up. "Get rid of my dishes. Tell him I had a sudden inspiration for a plot twist and can't be disturbed." She made a run for it and managed to get through the opening in the revolving library door before her eldest son came into the house.

Pushing it slowly shut, she blessed the smooth mechanism that uttered not a single scrape or squeak. Catching her in her robe in the kitchen wouldn't be so unusual. Only she knew she was naked under it.

But seeing her sitting there looking as if she'd just climbed out of bed when Andy's truck was parked out front... that would be exactly the fodder she'd just vowed not to feed her loving, exceedingly clever family.

15

Two mallets made a difference. So did the motivation provided by the sight of Desiree working across from him, pounding those logs into place with a rhythm that reminded him of something he'd rather be doing.

"Andy, you're slowing down. Need a break?"

"No, ma'am. Sorry. Got distracted."

"Did you, now?" She stopped pounding and gave him a knowing smile.

"Full disclosure, when you're diligently hammering away, a certain part of you that I'm fond of does a tempting cha-cha."

"In other words, I should have worn a sports bra."

"Not on my account."

"Hm." She studied him. "I spy the neck of a white T-shirt under that flannel."

"Yes, ma'am. It was at least fifteen degrees colder this morning, so I—"

"How about taking off your flannel shirt so I can enjoy your rippling biceps and flexing pecs while you hammer away?"

He grinned. "Fair enough." Laying down his mallet, he unbuttoned his shirt. "I'm lucky you didn't ask me to go shirtless so you can admire my chest hair."

"I considered it, except there's nothing sexy about a guy whose teeth are chattering." But there was something highly arousing about a guy unbuttoning his shirt, especially when he had a muscular chest to show off. She sucked in a breath.

Folding the shirt, he laid it on top of her toolbox. "Is that better?"

'Much." She gulped and reminded herself that Marybeth was baking pumpkin pies in the kitchen and Sky or Buck could pop in to check on their progress at any time.

"Backatcha, Dez," Andy said softly.

"Tonight seems like hours away."

He chuckled. "Because it is hours away. It's only been forty-five minutes since we finished lunch."

"Longest day ever."

"We're almost ready for the roof." He picked up his mallet. "Let's do this thing."

"First let me check my phone. I told Steven to text me when he's available to talk." She put down her mallet and walked over to the antique bar where they'd left their phones. "Fancy that. He texted fifteen minutes ago and said *anytime.*"

"Then I guess you might as well get it over with."

"Guess so." She gazed at him. "Wanna listen in?"

"Heck, yeah." He walked over to the bar.

"Then here goes." She tapped the phone.

It only rang once. Obviously the guy had been watching his phone.

"Hey, Desiree. Good to hear from you."

So effing jovial. Andy tensed. Maybe he shouldn't be listening if the sound of the dude's voice made him want to punch something.

"Hi, Steven." Desiree moved closer and laid her warm hand on his arm. "I have good news and more good news."

"That must mean you're willing to let me stay at the ranch house!"

That enthusiastic response clinched it in Andy's opinion. Grandpa #2 had Plans.

Desiree squeezed his arm. "Yes, you can stay here. There's no reason to put Maverick out of her room since I have space here."

"That was my thought. And bonus, she'll have grandma and grandpa in one place."

Andy gritted his teeth.

"Grandma and grandpas, plural."

"That's right! Can't forget good old Andy. Is he still running that little newspaper or is he eyeing retirement?"

"I doubt he'll be retiring anytime soon. In fact, on a personal note, Andy and I are seeing each other." She edged closer to him and held his gaze.

"Seeing each other? As in dating?"

"As in, he spends the night."

Andy blew her a kiss.

"With you?"

"Yes. And we're keeping it quiet, specifically not announcing it to the kids. Since you'll be staying here, I felt you needed to know. I'm sure I can trust you to respect our wishes and keep this information to yourself."

"Uh... well, sure... um, I'll do that, but... how long has this been going on?"

"A while." She grinned at Andy. "We have a lot in common, both being writers. I told him about M. R. Morrison."

"Kinda have to if he's sleeping with you. Well, I gotta go. Need to make an important call. See you on Tuesday."

"What time?"

"I land in Missoula in the morning, can't remember exactly when. I'll rent a car and text you when I'm on my way."

"Sounds good. 'Bye, Steven." She was laughing by the time she laid down the phone. "Classic!"

"You were awesome. C'mere." Pulling her into his arms, he kissed her. She let him, too, hugging him tight and whimpering when he took the kiss deeper.

He kept at it as long as he dared, craving the taste of her, but then he slowly loosened his grip and backed away, breathing hard. "Well done."

She laid a hand over her heaving chest. "Thanks." She sucked in air. "That was quite a reward, but now I need to call Beau and let him know Steven will be staying here."

"Go for it."

"I will, but if you're standing there watching me I might start giggling."

"Then I'll get back to work." He headed over to the playhouse and focused on the task while she assured Beau that this was the best plan for everyone.

Leaving her phone on the bar, she joined him at the playhouse and picked up her mallet. "I'd say it's official."

"What's that?"

"Steven's trip was primarily designed to win me back."

"Can't say I blame him." Andy gave one last tap to his current log and picked up another one. "In his shoes, I'd do the same. I'm surprised you don't have a constant parade of exes hoping for a second chance."

"I don't because we had an understanding that once they left, that was it. I only changed my mind once, with Bret and Gil's dad." She added another log on her side.

"Why him?"

"Circumstances, I guess. And the fact Derek's a rolling stone who likes variety."

"In women?"

"In women, his work schedule, where he lives, which meant I've never worried that he'll be clingy."

"Ah." Yeah, he'd been right to leave early last night. "What does he do?" Which was none of his business. "Never mind. You don't have to—"

"He flies small planes for tourist companies. He was working in Missoula and after we met, he spent his days off down here. That's when Bret was conceived. He left the state, but came back around the time I wanted another baby. Gil marked the end of our time together, although we're still friends."

The picture became clear. Bret and Molly had just welcomed baby Elvira. Desiree's friend Derek, the rolling stone, was another grandfather he might end up dealing with. "Does he know about Elvira?"

"Absolutely! He's tickled. He would have come for Christmas so he could see her, but he's hired on with an outfit in Sedona and this is their busy season. He'll probably show up next month sometime, so you'll get to meet him."

"Great." Yeah, he'd meet him all right. Who's to say Derek wouldn't take one look at Desiree and decide to bring that rolling stone to a dead stop? Flying tourists around could get old.

So could chasing acting gigs in various parts of the world. Cheyenne and Clint's dad Nick could retire any minute. On top of that, the grandbabies would keep coming, luring those retired grandpas back to Rowdy Ranch. As Desiree had pointed out, the baby routine was only beginning.

He'd identified everyone's dad except Rance's. Marsh's father Bill had attended Ella and Marsh's wedding in August and had brought his wife. No worries there. Desiree had adopted Lucky as a baby and his father was unknown.

While having the full roster would be helpful, asking about Rance's dad at this juncture would look like exactly what it was — a desire to complete a list of his potential competitors. Sure, he had home court advantage, but would that be enough?

He'd allow himself one more question and then move on. "Then Steven's the only one so far who's challenged the status quo?"

"Uh-huh. I wondered if he'd ever rethink his decision to leave thirty-two years ago. He was terrified that he'd beat up on Beau the way his dad beat up on him. Supposedly he loves traveling, but I wonder if that was ever true. Maybe he started running and didn't know how to stop."

"Oh." Well, damn. Now he felt sorry for the guy. "If you're right, that sucks."

"I have a hunch I am right." She continued to swing the mallet as she talked. "Coming to see Mav last year likely started the process of soul-searching and now he wants to make up for lost time. I'm sympathetic to that if he keeps his focus on Beau and Mav."

"Since you shut him down, he doesn't have much choice."

"Maybe narrowing his options is just what he needs." She paused, her expression thoughtful. Then she glanced at him, a light of inspiration flashing in her eyes. "He could learn a lot from you."

"Me?" That brought him to a halt, too. "Good old Andy who runs a little newspaper and probably should consider retiring?"

"He said that because he was trying to cut you down to size. He knew you'd be competition from the moment he met you last year. I'll bet you intimidate the hell out of him."

"Then let's keep it that way. I'm not a good mentor candidate, especially after what you just told him."

"I disagree. Sure, he's probably jealous and envious, but he also needs a friend. I can't be that friend because he still thinks of me in sexual terms."

"And I'm the guy who mucked up his plans for getting back with you. I can't see him wanting to spend two minutes with me, Dez, let alone become my best buddy."

"Did you see him last year with Mav? He fumbled around something terrible."

"She was a newborn. People get scared about holding newborns if they've never done it. She's older now. I'm sure he'll do much better."

"Especially if he has a role model."

He gazed across the space between them. "I want to be your knight in shining armor and slay dragons for you, but could you come up with a different dragon? Something easy, like solving world hunger?"

She smiled. "You think it's a terrible idea."

"Yes, I do."

"That's because you haven't let it percolate. Some of the best ideas sound crazy at first."

"And some of the worst ideas sound crazy at first because they are, in fact, crazy."

"You'll have a couple of days to think about it before he gets here. I'm betting you'll come to see this is a brilliant plan."

"You'll lose that bet." Or maybe not. He'd have a couple of days to think while she'd have three lusty nights to turn his brain to mush.

He had no desire to be pals with Grandpa #2. But a man would be a fool to underestimate the power of persuasion wielded by Desiree McLintock.

<u>16</u>

"It's really awesome." Desiree stood with Andy, Marybeth, Buck, Sky and Sam as they all admired the finished playhouse. She'd waited for Andy to put his shirt on before she'd texted them and invited them to come see it.

"Terrific job, you two." Sky turned and gave her a hug and traded high-fives with Andy. "I hope you realize this sets a precedent. Susie needs one next Christmas."

"I'm up for it," Andy said. "Now that we've done this one, the next time will be a breeze."

"If you build one for Susie you'd better check with Cheyenne and Kendall." Marybeth walked around to the back of the playhouse to check out the windows. "I'm guessing they'll want Jodie to have one, too."

Desiree laughed. "Log cabin playhouses all around. I love it."

"I'm impressed with the quality." Buck opened and closed the front door. "That's gonna last."

Andy nodded. "I think so, too. I can't wait for Jess and Beau to see it."

"You could text them a picture," Marybeth said.

"Great idea, but I'm not taking the chance. That little munchkin is already fascinated by cell phones. She's liable to be there when the image comes through."

"She recognizes that ping." Desiree glanced at him. "And when she hears it—"

"She *insists* on seeing what's on the screen."

"Yes, she does." Desiree chuckled. "Even if it's a text she can't read."

"Guaranteed she'll read early, though."

"That's a given, considering..." She paused, suddenly aware that the other three people in the room hadn't contributed to that exchange. Instead they stood gazing at them and smiling. "Excuse the doting grandparents. We get carried away."

"You're allowed." Sky's expression was slightly different from the other two. His smile was just as indulgent, but speculation flickered briefly in his eyes as he glanced from her to Andy.

Uh-oh. "Well, folks, thanks for coming in to admire the results of our labor. I'm sure everyone has things to do. You'll be shocked to hear that tomorrow's Christmas Eve Day."

"Cheyenne and I are picking up the flatbed first thing in the morning," Sky said. "Angie and Kendall are coming over to attach the lights to the sleigh and the harness around ten. They'll also braid Thor's mane and tail. We plan on pulling out of here with the flatbed and the horse trailer around three."

"Sounds like you have it under control, son. Has anybody checked the weather report recently?"

"I have," Buck said. "They're predicting flurries but not an actual storm."

"That would be perfect. I hope that prediction holds up. You and Marybeth are riding in with me tomorrow evening, right?"

"We were planning on it," Marybeth said, "but we can drive ourselves if that would be more convenient."

"By all means, ride in with me. No reason to take two trucks." She wished Marybeth hadn't said that in front of Sky. She meant well, but she'd just given him another hint that something might be going on. Staying under the radar wouldn't be easy, but she'd known that.

"Okay, then. What time?"

"The gang's dinner reservation at the Buffalo is for six o'clock, so let's leave at five-fifteen."

"Got it."

"I'll meet you guys there tomorrow night," Andy said. "I plan to spend the day wrapping gifts. I've procrastinated, so I should probably take off now so I can get a head start on it."

He was leaving? That hadn't been the plan, but she'd trust in his ability to navigate this tricky situation.

"Before you take off," Sky said, "I know I speak for all my siblings when I say how grateful we are that you've kept Mom's secret all these years. We're happy and relieved to finally have it out in the open."

"I'm happy, too, Sky. Now I can geek out about her books, find out what research sources she's used, and how she plots the books."

"That's easy, I don't."

"Which makes them even more amazing. The plots are so tight, so intricate." He glanced at her. "We'll have plenty to talk about next time we get together. This playhouse has been a good thing in so many ways."

"Absolutely." She managed to keep a straight face. "Have a safe drive home."

"Thanks. See you all later." Picking up his rubber mallet and the small toolbox they'd never opened, and he walked out of the room.

Sam stood gazing after him. Then with a quick backward glance at her, he trotted after his new best friend.

"We'd better get going, too," Marybeth said. "We also haven't finished wrapping. Let's vamoose, Buck." She gestured to him and started toward the door. Then she turned back. "I made a couple of individual pumpkin pies. I know you won't cut into the big ones when it's only you eating it."

"Thanks, Marybeth. I do hate to take just one slice. Now I have desert for tonight. My mouth's been watering all day smelling them baking."

"Mine, too. I made a couple for Buck and me. See you tomorrow!"

"We'll have some big fun!" she called after them. Then she glanced at Sky. "I appreciate you and Cheyenne organizing the sleigh ride."

"It'll be a blast. We'll all take turns driving it, so with ten of us, it'll be a piece of cake."

"Even Clint and Rance? Won't they be swamped at the Buffalo?"

"Tyra's gonna fill in for them so they can each take a turn. They're both such hams it would be wrong not to let them do it."

"Yeah, it would." She smiled. "The annual McLintock family sleighride begins tomorrow night. A tradition is born. Now we'll see how long we can keep it going."

"As long as I'm around we'll be doing it. I get the impression everyone else feels the same. What a great way to raise a little money and have a lot of fun."

"That's for sure. Oh, look. Sam decided to come back and find out if I'm still here." She smoothed a hand over the collie's silky head.

Sky put on his hat. "I need to get home. It's Susie's bath time and I love being part of that."

"Then get on out of here, cowboy. I'll walk you to the door."

"Hang on. I'd better take a picture of the playhouse to show Penny." He pulled out his phone and snapped several from different angles. "Impressive, Mom. You and Andy make a good team."

"Thanks." She walked toward the swinging bar doors.

Sky got ahead of her and held them open. "As you might guess, the texts have been flying today. Jess said Andy deliberately set this up so he could be alone with you."

"Yes, he did." She took a breath as they continued down the hall and into the kitchen. "That said, we—"

"He's in love with you. Everybody can see that. And you seem fond of him."

"Who wouldn't be? He's a great guy."

"The best." They reached the entry and he paused. "I've been appointed to tell you that we respect your privacy. Yours and Andy's. We won't bug you guys."

"Thank you."

"You're so strong, Mom, and the most independent woman we know. We all love that about you. And we also wanna say, if you're ever going to take that leap, you'll never do better than Andy Hartmann."

She met his steady gaze. "I know that, son. That's why I'm treading very carefully."

"Love you." He hugged her.

"Love you, too. Now git."

"Yes, ma'am." Touching two fingers to the brim of his hat, he opened the front door and stepped out.

She took hold of the door as his long strides took him across the porch. "Give Susie a kiss for me!"

"Always!" he called over his shoulder as he clattered down the steps.

She stood, not minding the cold as she watched him walk to the truck, the multicolored Christmas lights in the trees bathing him in rainbows. Sky. Her firstborn, Charley's son, who looked so much like him.

Slowly she closed the door, turned around and leaned against it.

Sky was the only person besides Marybeth who had an inkling of the bond she'd shared with that wonderful man. Charley was the yardstick by which she'd measured every man since then. None of them had measured up.

Until now.

Sam nudged her leg and she slid down to sit on the floor. Flopping down beside her, Sam laid his head in her lap.

"Andy scares the hell out of me, Sam." She combed her fingers through his ruff. "When I lost Charley, I promised myself if I ever found someone as kind, smart, ethical and funny as Charley, I'd marry him. I didn't think that would ever happen."

Sam let out a doggie sigh.

"Exactly. I'm screwed. Andy's proven he's good at the husband gig but I might as well face facts. I'd make a terrible wife. I'm bossy and opinionated."

Sam raised his head and looked up at her.

"Yeah, you know what I'm like. Always giving you orders. I'm used to making decisions without consulting anybody. I'm used to saying *I*, not *we.* I—"

Sam scrambled to his feet and took off, heading for the library.

"What the hell?" Jumping up, she followed him. She was halfway through her office and Sam had made it into her bedroom when the back door swung open.

Andy stood in the shaft of light looking adorably startled. "Damn, that's cool. Sorry if I scared you, but I didn't know if I should text, or—"

"You found it. I thought you'd need me to show you."

"You described it well." He walked in and turned around, gazing at the opening. "But when I saw the solid wall I began to doubt myself. How do you close it?"

"Click the red button."

"Makes sense, but I wasn't going to push it until I knew. It might be the panic button." He tapped it with his thumb and the door swung shut. "Wow, you can't see it from this side, either. Who did you say put this in for you?"

"Gene, Angie's dad."

"Incredible workmanship." Pocketing the key fob, he turned back to her and smiled. "Hi."

She dragged in a breath. "I've thought it through."

"Oh?"

"You're terrific husband material and that's totally wasted on me. I don't have what it takes to be a good wife and I never will. We should give this up as a bad job."

17

"Where did that come from?" Andy gazed at her in confusion. "Twenty minutes ago we were exchanging happy talk about the playhouse and Mav's phone obsession. Four hours ago you were kissing me like there's no tomorrow. What gives, Dez?"

"The kids have been communicating all day about our situation. They deputized Sky to tell me that they'll respect our privacy and not bug us."

"That's good news, right?"

"They also want me to know that if I'm ever going to *take the leap* as Sky put it, I'll never do better than you."

He groaned. After he'd worked so hard not to trigger her marriage phobia, her awesome but misguided kids had set her off while he wasn't around to initiate damage control.

"I'm never going to take that leap, Andy. It would be easy-peasy for you. You were married for years and clearly were good at it. Mary adored you."

Might as well meet this head-on. "Are you saying you want your key fob back?"

She gulped. "Wouldn't that be for the best?"

"No."

"Think about it. You were happily married for a huge chunk of your life. You say you're not interested in marrying me but I question that."

"Which means I'm either lying or I don't know my own mind?"

She hesitated. "I wouldn't put it that way."

"You sorta did. Wanna know why I'm not interested in marrying you?"

"Yes, I do."

"Because you're not interested in marrying me. Or anyone. It's not personal, so I'm not insulted. I am interested in being with you, either in a crowd when it's family time, or in your arms when it's not. The prospect of that puts a smile on my face. End of story."

"You make it sound so simple."

"Because it is. Would the kids like to see us take that trip down the aisle? Of course they would. They're in that mode themselves so why wouldn't they think like that?"

"But you don't?"

"Not unless you do a one-eighty on the subject. I fully admit if you asked me to marry you, I'd say yes."

"Aha! And you're hoping I will."

"Not at all. I'm hoping you'll invite me to take off my coat and stay awhile."

The corners of her mouth tipped up. A good sign. "Marybeth made us two individual pumpkin pies."

"I can't believe you'd tell me that and then ask for your key fob."

"That would be mean."

"Should I take off my coat?"

"Yes, please."

"My hat?"

"That, too."

He laid them on the easy chair by the fireplace. "My shirt?"

"Might as well." She grinned and started unbuttoning hers.

Game over. Even Sam knew it. He walked to his bed and flopped down.

Clothes went flying as they stripped off everything and tossed it, once again, on the floor.

"Move it, slowpoke." She raced naked to the bed.

"I'm working around an impediment."

"Excuses, excuses." Pillows scattered and the covers whooshed as she flipped them to the foot of the bed. "Let's see some action."

He kicked aside his jeans, said to hell with his socks and grabbed her before she could jump onto the wide, snowy expanse. "Gotcha, smarty pants." Wrapping his arms around her waist, he pulled her against his chest, leaned down and nipped the curve of her neck.

She squealed. "Andy Hartmann, did you just give me a hickey?"

"Hope so. Maybe I should try again just to make sure."

"Don't you dare, you crazy man."

"But you're so tempting, so delicious." Nuzzling the spot, he slid his hand between her thighs and sent his fingers on a fact-finding mission. Ahhh. Nice.

With a soft moan, she sank back against him, giving him greater access.

He put his mouth close to her ear. "Interesting response from a woman who was ready to send me out the door."

She gulped. "Never said I didn't want you."

"Then let's concentrate on that for now." He pushed deeper, stroking slowly while he teased her with his thumb.

She gasped, her muscles clenching. "We should... we should get into..."

"We will." He nibbled on her earlobe. "In a minute."

She didn't need the full minute. In seconds she came, panting and trembling as he braced her against his chest, closed his eyes and said a prayer of thanks. Crisis averted.

"That was lovely." She took a shaky breath. "I'd like to crawl into bed now, please."

"Let me help." Slipping his hand free, he hooked his arm under her knees and lifted her onto the mattress. Then he reached down and pulled off his socks, one by one.

"What are you doing?"

"Taking off my socks."

"You didn't before?"

"Didn't have time. The clock was ticking."

"What clock?"

"Yours. You wanted to see some action and I decided the socks could wait."

She smiled. "You're adorable." Then her gaze lowered. "I think your clock is ticking."

"Nice of you to notice."

"Then come get me." She rolled to the center of the bed and held out her arms. "I'm all yours."

The phrase hit a soft spot in his heart. Made his breath hitch. Probably wouldn't be the last time that happened, either.

He didn't need a wedding ring on her finger. But did he want her to love him forever and ever, amen? Yes, he did.

One day at a time, dude. One day at a time. He climbed onto that perfect mattress that wasn't too soft and wasn't too firm. Palms flat, arms straight, he braced himself above the woman who'd stolen his heart.

She gazed up at him with a soft smile, as if she liked what she saw. He sure did. She was incandescent. "I'm a very lucky guy."

She brushed her fingers lightly over his chest. "I'd say you make your own luck. I admire that about you, Andy."

"And my chest hair."

She smiled. "Uh-huh."

Probing gently, he slowly eased his cock in and watched her eyes change color. Gradually they darkened until they were almost green. Last night he'd been too busy controlling his climax to savor this moment.

Her lips parted and a flush rose to her cheeks. "I like this."

"Good. Me, too."

Sliding her hands around his waist, she hugged him closer. "Don't forget—"

"I won't." Holding her gaze, he put his weight on his forearms and sank down until his chest touched hers. Then he began to move.

She exhaled, a long, slow sigh of pleasure. "Heaven."

"Yes, ma'am."

"It just doesn't get any better than this."

"Oh, yes, it does." He added a slight hip rotation to each stroke.

Her eyes widened. "Oh, my."

"Good?"

"Yep."

He picked up the pace, found his rhythm. This was more like it — no insecure internal babbling, just loving a fantastic lady who was loving him back, rising to meet him, eagerness in her touch as she gripped his butt and hung on.

She was into this, into him. He wallowed in the joy of it, held back his release — not because he was afraid she wouldn't come. She would. But because this was so damned amazing he wanted it to last.

Her breath quickened, adding to the stimulation of his chest rubbing against hers. When she breathed in, her tight nipples stroked his sensitive skin. She was close. So was he.

She gave a quick gasp as her first spasm hit. "Together?"

Her murmured request went straight to his privates. "Together." When she cried out and arched into him, he pushed deep and let go, melding with her, breathing out when she breathed in, his gaze locked with hers.

She stayed with him, didn't turn her head or close her eyes. The open, trusting glow in those eyes humbled him. He'd strive to be worthy of it.

Slowly her body relaxed. She continued to maintain eye contact, though. "Keeps getting better."

"That's the idea."

She took a breath. "But— oh, never mind."

"What?" He had a hunch.

"It wasn't a helpful comment."

"Can I take a guess?"

Her eyebrows lifted. "You think you know?"

"Maybe. Was it about the law of diminishing returns?"

"Along those lines. I mean, realistically...."

"Depends."

She searched his gaze, questions brimming in hers.

"You can ask me anything, Dez."

"Not anything."

"Yes, you can. It's okay."

"Did it... did it keep getting better?"

"Yes."

She swallowed and hugged him tight. "I wish she'd lived."

"So do I. But she didn't." He hesitated. Yeah, now might be the time. "She told me to get back out there. Made me promise."

"I hadn't heard that. Did she set a timeline?"

"No, thank God."

"Then I'm helping you keep your promise?"

"Yes, ma'am."

_18_

Spending time in bed with Andy made Desiree forget about dinner, but Sam didn't forget. He got them moving, which was probably a good thing. A girl couldn't survive on sex alone, although Andy's skill made her tempted to try.

Working side by side in her kitchen, they fed the dog, warmed the soup, made toasted cheese sandwiches and opened the second bottle of wine. She'd left out the large tray he'd used to bring dinner in the night before and they had it loaded with food and wine glasses when she remembered Sam needed to go out.

"I'll take him. I'm dressed."

He had her there. She was wearing nothing but her fluffy purple robe. "Thanks, but you're barefoot."

"I'll just go fetch my boots."

"Or you could put on a pair of snow boots from the hall closet."

"Even better. Come on, pup."

"While you do that, I'll carry the tray in. You can bring the wine."

"Will do," he called over his shoulder.

"See you soon." Hefting the tray, she made her way toward the bedroom, smiling at Andy's one-sided conversation with Sam as he sorted through the snow boot selection.

He and Mary used to have dogs — goldens, as she recalled. Made sense that Andy would feel right at home dealing with Sam.

Setting the tray on a small but sturdy table in front of the beehive fireplace, she opened the flue, grabbed a box of matches and lit the balled-up newspapers under the grate.

During moments like this, when she and Andy were apart, she had mixed emotions about accepting what he so generously gave. But when he held her in his arms, those doubts went out the window.

It wasn't just sex, either, although he certainly had a talent for that. He also had truckloads of empathy, a gift for putting himself in someone else's shoes and making them feel heard and understood. That was precious and she lapped it up.

The fire caught, for which she was grateful. It was mainly for atmosphere and she didn't want to have to fool with it. Speaking of atmosphere, she might want to tidy up.

She pulled up the covers, folded them back and grabbed the pillows off the floor. Andy was wearing his clothes, but hers lay scattered. Snatching them up, she carried them to the clothes hamper in the bathroom.

"Looks great," Andy called out. "Do I get to sit in your lap?"

"That could make eating dinner a challenge, but I'm up for it if you are." She walked back into her bedroom. Damn, but he looked good standing in it, his cheeks ruddy from the cold.

"I vote we don't try it. Chances are we'd start fooling around and get soup and toasted cheese all over your beautiful chair. I'll haul one in here if you'll tell me which one you want."

"How about my purple wingback? I'll sit in that and you can have this one." She gestured to the easy chair in front of the fireplace.

"Works for me." He handed her the open bottle of wine. "Sam, go lie down. You had your dinner. That's for us."

The collie gazed up at him, tail wagging.

"No more treats. Go lie down." He gestured toward the dog bed and Sam sauntered over and plopped down.

She grinned. "I can't believe you gave him a treat for going outside to do his business."

"It's cold out there. He didn't wanna."

"Sucker."

"Dogs and kids. What can I say?"

"You're a softie." Walking over to the tray, she poured them each a glass of wine and then set the bottle on her dresser. "But if you keep giving him treats you'll need to go outside and play with him so he doesn't get fat."

"I'd love to." The yearning in his voice came through loud and clear.

Her breath caught. What had she been thinking? She turned, scrambling for the right words.

His gaze was steady. "But that would involve me coming over during the day and hanging out, wouldn't it?"

"Guess so." Her heart thundered. She'd worried that he'd take up too much space in her life. Here was a perfect example of how that could happen. So why was the image of him playing in the snow with Sam so appealing?

"I'll go get the chair."

When he came back carrying her purple wingback, she was still standing there trying to come up with the right thing to say. She adored him. Hurting him was the last thing she wanted.

He set the chair aside, crossed to her and drew her into his arms. "Don't freak out, Dez."

"I'm not. I just—"

"You didn't mean to open that door."

Lifting her head, she looked into his eyes. "You're right, I didn't, but... it would be nice taking Sam out together. I'm sure we'd have fun. On the other hand, I...." She trailed off, not ready to put words to the thoughts swirling in her head.

"On the other hand, you've established a pattern that works for you." He gently massaged her back.

She nodded. "Angie's dad was the last man who lived with me in this house. That was twenty-five years ago."

"And the house was full of people then. It's a wonder you got any writing done."

"Yet that was a highly productive time, mostly thanks to Buck and Marybeth. They wouldn't let the kids interrupt me unless there was blood."

"Which probably happened a lot when you had ten kids running around."

"It did. But we made it through." She slipped her arms around his neck. "And now the house is often empty except for me and Sam. And that's okay."

His jaw firmed. "I'll stop giving him extra treats."

"That's not the—"

"I know, but it's a fact that he needs more exercise if I'm feeding him treats. I can't exercise him unless we decide to go public. And we can't do that until we've figured out what this is."

"Are you saying it's not quite as simple as you thought?"

His smile was almost a grimace. "Yeah, okay, it's not." He sighed and pulled her closer. "But some of it is. Like eating a delicious meal in front of the fireplace and then making love in that big old bed. Nothing complicated going on there."

"So much for my plan to bust out my copy of the *Kama Sutra*."

His eyebrows rose. "And she throws down the gauntlet."

"Not really. I was kidding."

"Do you even have a copy?"

"Somewhere. Derek gave it to me as a joke. Which is doubly funny because he's not a reader."

"I seriously doubt it was a joke. When a man gives a woman the *Kama Sutra* he's hoping for some creative action."

"You know this from personal experience?"

"Sadly, I do not. I always meant to buy a copy and never did. But trust me on this. He was hoping you'd suggest thumbing through it and trying some of those poses."

"Then he should have said something. I just laughed and shoved it in a bookcase, thinking I might use it as a joke present someday, myself. Then I never did. Anyway, we should eat while the food's hot."

"Right." He released her. "I'll move your chair."

While he positioned it on the far side of the little table, she used the fireplace tongs to shift the logs slightly so they'd burn brighter and faster.

"Nice fire."

"I wanted it to be big enough to be cozy and small enough to be coals by the time we finish eating."

"Looks about right for that." He gestured to her chair. "Milady."

"Thanks." She settled into it and he took the armchair. Picking up her wine glass, she held it in his direction. "To simplicity."

"I can't drink to that. I'm still thinking about the *Kama Sutra*."

"Me and my big mouth."

"I love it when you talk dirty."

She blew out a breath. "Are you going to be a PITA about this book?"

"I think so. I'd forgotten about it, but now I'm motivated to finally get a look at the thing."

"Just look at it?"

"Clearly you haven't been paying attention. I want to look and then experiment."

"What if I don't want to?"

"You say you don't, but I'll bet you'll change your mind when you see the pictures. Which bookcase?"

"I'm not telling you. Do you have an alternate toast since you don't like mine?"

"How about *to creativity.*"

"Just creativity in general?"

"Um, sure."

"All right. To creativity." She tapped her wine glass against his.

"And what's the ultimate creative act? Having sex."

"I knew it. You were drinking to the *Kama Sutra.*"

"I can't believe you don't secretly want to page through it with me."

"Not really. The whole turning yourselves into a pretzel approach doesn't appeal to me. I'm very happy with how we've progressed so far."

"Is it in the library or in your office?"

"That's for me to know and you to find out."

"Which I will, given enough time and opportunity."

"I'm gonna keep you so busy you won't have either."

"Doing what?"

"Take a guess."

He laughed. "Win-win."

19

Andy was curious about the *Kama Sutra* the way he was curious about anything he'd never seen before, like the Taj Mahal and elephants in the wild. But he wasn't as obsessed as he'd led Desiree to believe.

Then again, if he could get his hands on it and they tried a position or two, he'd be one up on hot-shot pilot Derek. He'd loved hearing that she'd shelved the book instead of diving into the contents with that dude.

And there it was. He'd officially reverted to his high school days as a young stud, when he'd focused on obliterating the competition. That was funny.

"What're you chuckling about over there?"

"Me. I'm behaving like an eighteen-year-old."

"If it's regarding the *Kama Sutra*, I completely agree. You're like a kid searching under his parents' bed for *Playboy*."

"It's not really the book I'm after." He dipped a corner of his toasted cheese sandwich in the soup and took a bite.

"Then what is it?"

He finished chewing and swallowed. "It's a chance to get one up on your ex."

Her eyes widened and she almost choked on her wine. Swallowing quickly, she went through a fit of coughing and laughing that made her eyes water.

"You okay?" He put his sandwich plate and soup bowl back on the tray in case she needed help.

Patting her chest, she gave him a hoarse *yeah.* Then she cleared her throat a couple of times. "What a riot." She wiped her eyes with her napkin and turned to him. "You see *Derek* as competition?"

"Looks like it."

"I knew you had an issue with Steven, but it didn't occur to me that you'd think Derek...." She trailed off, gazing at him with a bemused smile. "That explains the timing of the dancing lessons with Clint back in February."

"Yes, ma'am. It was torture seeing you looking so happy out there on the floor with Nick. And I figured he'd be coming back now that he has a grandbaby to spoil."

"He will. He's dying to see Jodi, but he can't leave Australia until the movie wraps."

"That's too bad."

She started laughing again.

"No, I mean it. She's adorable and soon she'll be crawling. I've loved every stage with Mav and Nick's already missed stuff."

"That's kind of you to say."

"I like the guy. His visits make Cheyenne and Clint happy. But I get twitchy when he flirts with you."

"Would it help to know I have the same issue with the flirting? And that goes for any of the dads."

"Yes, ma'am. I want to hear all about it." He dipped his sandwich in the soup again. "You should try this. It's even better than just plain bread."

"I will, right after I calm your fears, starting with Derek. Why do you consider him competition?"

He paused, the dripping sandwich halfway to his mouth. "He's a pilot. That's a sexy job. Plus I overheard Bret and Gil mention he's a bodybuilder. And number one on the list, he's single." He bit into the sandwich.

"I'll admit the pilot thing was a draw in the beginning. The flyboy allure wore off pretty quick."

He nodded, pleased with that news.

"As for his muscles, the boys are probably remembering the times he took them swimming in the creek when they were kids. I doubt he still looks like that, although I don't know for sure. The last time I saw him naked was almost thirty years ago."

Shoving that image right out of his head, he kept chewing.

"Sorry."

He quickly swallowed. "No worries. It's fine."

"You winced."

"I know and I'm being ridiculous. We each have a sexual past. It's not like Mary was my first."

"Are you in touch with any of your ex-girlfriends?"

"One contacted me a year or so after Mary died. Offered to fly out for a visit. I politely told her that wouldn't work for me."

"Too soon?"

"For me it was, but I kept her number in case I changed my mind."

Her breathing hitched. "Still have it?"

Aha. Maybe he wasn't the only one bedeviled by the green monster. "I deleted it from my phone the day after Mav was born."

"Oh." The corners of her mouth tipped up.

He'd given her the right answer. "There's something I need to remember about the men in your life. I'm here and they're not."

"Excellent point. Also, you've overlooked the key element of Derek's story, something I told you first thing. C'mon, Sherlock. Find the clue."

Sipping his wine, he replayed the conversation. Ahh, there it was, the reason Bret and Gil's dad had never been in the running. "He's not a reader."

"Bingo. He only reads when he has no choice. He's intelligent, a quality I insisted on for my children's sake, but he's not intellectually curious. Aside from the weather, we literally had nothing to talk about except Bret and Gil. Zach and Elvira will expand the conversational possibilities, but you get the gist."

"When did you find out he hates to read?"

"Fairly early. I was already pregnant with Bret, though, which meant I was writing up a storm and didn't have time for long discussions with anyone. It didn't matter that we didn't talk much."

"Wait. Are you saying pregnancy was *good* for your writing? I would have thought the opposite."

"Being pregnant was jet fuel for my muse. Since giving birth was easy and I wanted lots of kids, I spent seven years having babies and releasing a bunch of books."

"I never put those two things together."

"Check the copyright dates. The momentum put me on the bestseller lists and I've managed to stay there even though my production slowed down after Angie was born."

"That's fascinating. I wish... well, no, I don't, not really, but to be part of that — immersed in sex, babies, and creativity — I get hot just thinking about it."

She smiled. "And would you have been willing to father nine kids in seven years? Plus adopt another along the way?"

"That would have been daunting. At least for me."

"It is for most men. When I met Bill, Marsh's dad, I had two toddlers and a set of infant twins. He was fine with giving me another baby, but he had no desire to stick around when I told him I wanted more after that."

"Which made Derek a logical choice."

"Exactly. He was never gonna stay. It's possible Angie's dad would have liked to, since I told him I was out of the baby business now that I had a daughter and my career was going great."

"Would you have let him stay?"

"Maybe. He was a good guy. But we never talked about it and...."

"Yep. Shit happens." He held her gaze. She hadn't been with Angie's dad for very long, but his death had exacted a toll. He could see it in her eyes. "Did you love him?"

"I loved all of them."

That took him aback.

"Does it shock you to hear me say it?"

"A little. Since you didn't consider asking them to stick around until the last one, I figured you weren't that attached."

"You can love someone without wanting to be with them forever."

"I suppose so." He sorted through that statement to find out if there was a message for him embedded in it. He hoped not.

"They were willing to give me the precious gift of a child with their DNA. Nick and Derek each gave me two. That would be enough for me to love them, but they are all decent guys, kind and generous. I was happy to have them visit, with the understanding we wouldn't be having sex anymore."

"They didn't protest that rule?"

"Nah. They'd moved on, found girlfriends, tried marriage. Bill's the only one who made it work. The others are all single, now, which I didn't expect."

His unease returned.

"I thought they'd all get married and have families of their own. Instead I have a bunch of single grandpas eager to bond with their Rowdy Ranch grandbabies."

"And Rowdy Ranch's single grandma?"

She made a face. "Let's hope Steven's an outlier and not the tip of the iceberg." She paused. "Have you given any more thought to befriending him while he's here?"

Resistance tightened his chest.

"You still don't like the concept."

"But you do."

"Of course. It was my idea."

"While I understand his behavior better after what you've told me, I have trouble with his decision to stay away for more than thirty years. Beau struggled with that."

"He did."

"I've been a fan of that boy for years, ever since he rescued those pot-bellied pigs from a hoarding situation and found them homes. He has a tender heart, and when I discovered how Steven basically ignored—"

"You're right. He should have faced his demons long ago. I'm guessing he still has a lot to learn."

"And you want him to learn those things because you love him."

She met his gaze, her eyes luminous. "I do. I also love Beau, Jess and Mav. Steven doesn't know the first thing about fitting into a family unit and you're a pro at it."

He smiled. "Flattery will get you everywhere."

"It's not flattery. You—"

"Dez, he won't want to be friends with me."

"Since when has that been a hurdle you can't jump?" Reaching across the table, she squeezed his arm. "Turn on your Andy charm over a couple of beers. You'll soften him right up."

"I do believe someone's turned on her Desiree charm."

"Is it working?"

"Yes, ma'am, although you haven't softened me up. You've inspired a completely different reaction."

She glanced at their empty soup bowls and sandwich plates. "Since we seem to be finished here, would you like to do something about that reaction?"

"Is there a catch with Steven's name on it?" Not that it mattered. She'd roped him in.

"No catch. Do whatever you feel is right."

He laughed. "I'll take him under my wing, just like you knew I would."

"Thank you." She stood and held out her hand. "Come to bed. I'm craving some of that Andy charm."

20

"Cuddling after sex is good." Desiree lay sprawled over Andy, her cheek resting on his chest. He'd turned her inside out once again, leaving her limp, sweaty and satisfied.

"Sure is." He stroked her hip. "Makes me sleepy, though, and I don't want to fall asleep."

"Me, either. We still have those individual pumpkin pies Marybeth left us."

"Oh, yeah. I forgot about those." He chuckled, making his chest vibrate. "Wonder why."

"Can't imagine." She rubbed her cheek over his silky chest hair, then turned her head so she could lay a kiss on the spot where his heart beat a steady rhythm.

The jury was in. She'd told Marybeth she was a little bit in love with him. No more. She was all the way in, at least up to her neck, maybe even over her head.

"The Christmas tree lights give off a really nice glow."

"Uh-huh."

"Do you leave them on all night?"

"I did last night. They remind me of you. Makes me feel cozy."

"I would think they'd keep you awake, though."

"They sort of do, but that's okay."

He bunched a pillow under his head. "So if I stayed, you'd turn them off and get some sleep?"

"That's a silly reason to stay. You made a good point about why it's better if you—"

"I'm staying."

"Andy." Propping herself on her elbows, she gave him her best disapproving face. "No, you're not. If you're concerned about me leaving the lights on, I'll turn them off."

He smiled. "Good, because they'd keep me awake for sure."

"Listen, buster, you're not—"

"What if I want to stay?"

"But last night you said it was a problem."

"And then I drove home missing you like crazy, and when I climbed into my own, very cold bed, I had a hell of a time going to sleep. I just lay there wishing I hadn't left."

The warmth in his gaze sent a river of happiness flowing through her. "Then I guess you'd better stay."

"We'll both get more sleep."

"Which makes it a practical decision."

His eyes twinkled. "Absolutely."

"I'll set my special alarm. You'll love it."

"Hard to imagine loving an alarm, especially when it means I'm leaving you."

His romantic words and the huskiness in his voice arrowed right into her heart. "I hope you know we're falling for each other."

"Speak for yourself. I fell a long time ago."

She sucked in a breath. "Me, too."

"Does it scare you?"

"Uh-huh. A little. You?"

"I'm terrified."

"Really? Of what?"

"That I'll screw it up, be too clingy."

"I can't picture you being clingy."

"Why not? I just admitted I spent hours pining for you last night."

"That's romantic. Flattering."

"Hm. So what's your definition of clingy?"

"Annoying attachment. Hanging around when it's clear the person wants some space. You wouldn't do that. You're emotionally tuned in." She scooted up so his mouth was within range of hers.

"You must be, too." He cupped the back of her head. "Because I desperately need a kiss."

"Comin' atcha." Leaning closer, she eased into the kiss, relaxing her lips, sliding her tongue into his mouth.

With a groan, he rolled her to her back and moved between her thighs. One swift thrust and he was there, carrying her away on a rhythmic journey as natural as breathing.

She wrapped him in her arms and surrendered to the gentle ebb and flow, the tension building in her core, the warmth of his skin, the hunger of his kiss.

Then he paused, lifted his lips from hers and issued a gruff command. "Look at me."

Her gaze locked with his. The intensity in the depths of his blue eyes sent a jolt of electricity through her.

"I love you, Dez."

She swallowed. Took a shaky breath. "I love you, too. And I don't know what to do about it."

"You don't have to do anything." His expression softened. "Except love me back."

"Seems I can't help it."

"It's enough." He began to move again, faster, now. Then he bore down, stroking with intent until she let go. So did he, driving in one last time, his body shuddering, his words coming between gasps. "More... than... enough."

* * *

Andy's absence the next day as Desiree wrapped gifts and completed last-minute tasks created an unsettling void. Several times she resisted the urge to call him on some pretext just to hear his voice.

Meanwhile his declaration of love played in her head, causing her to flush with pleasure. She impatiently awaited the Christmas Eve meal at the Buffalo when she'd see him again.

Might as well face it. She was stuck on Andy Hartmann in a way she hadn't been stuck on anyone except... yep. Charley Fox.

Which presented a problem. Her kids had never seen her in such an addled state. They'd witnessed fondness and affection toward the men who'd temporarily shared her life. She'd loved all those guys and still did, but not like this.

As the afternoon ticked away, eagerness and anxiety took turns jumping around in her stomach. Playing it cool in front of her children and children-in-law had sounded easy twenty-four hours ago.

But after last night... how in hell was she supposed to hide this massive crush? How could she get control of her runaway emotions?

But she had to, not only for her kids' sake but for Andy's. He could make logical assumptions. Women who were this crazy about a man had to be dying to make a commitment, right?

And here was the scariest part — while she knew beyond a shadow of a doubt that she wasn't marriage material, a part of her *wanted* to be. Something was seriously wrong for her to be thinking that way.

She spent so much time getting ready that she barely made it out the door by the five-fifteen departure she'd set. Buck and Marybeth were right on time, bundled up against the cold and wearing happy smiles as they climbed into her truck.

Although she chatted with them all the way into town, she couldn't have recapped the conversation if someone paid her. Was Andy there yet? How would he greet her? How should she greet him? Would seeing him settle her down or jack her up even more?

She lucked out and found a parking space not far from the Buffalo's front door. Andy's gray truck was closer, indicating he'd arrived early. Beau's dark red one sat next to it. Andy was probably out on the dance floor with Mav, who loved being whirled around in time with the music.

"I'll bet the buffalo's greeting will be different tonight," Marybeth said as they walked up the sidewalk toward the entrance. "Seems to me it changes more often these days."

"Whoever's making those recordings is having a good time with them." Desiree had spent years trying to solve the mystery of who it was. Had Andy solved it? Now she could picture him figuring it out and not telling anyone.

Buck opened the door and held it as a country version of *Run Run Rudolph* spilled out into the cold night air. "After you, ladies."

Marybeth waved her in with a murmured *go find that man*.

She gave Marybeth a startled look and got a wink in return. If Marybeth had guessed she was twitterpated over Andy, then so would the rest of her family. She did *not* want that.

Squaring her shoulders, she took a deep breath and walked past the large wooden buffalo wearing a Santa hat.

Haaaapyyy Chriiiistmaaas Eeeeve, y'aaaall, the buffalo moaned.

"Told you it would be a new one!" Marybeth sauntered through and set off the recording a second time.

Desiree took several steps into the crowded tavern overflowing with music, laughter, twinkling lights, red bows, and evergreen accents. She scanned the room with pretended nonchalance.

There he was. The noise and color faded. All that mattered was the broad-shouldered man spinning Mav around the dance floor. He laughed as she patted his cheeks and bounced in his arms.

Distance kept her from hearing his low chuckle of delight. Didn't matter. That delicious sound was stored deep in her soul, along with the warmth of his smile and the brush of his hand over her skin. She crossed her arms to hide an involuntary quiver.

"They look cute out there." Marybeth stood beside her.

"They do." Her cheeks heated. Couldn't control that, or the rapid beat of her heart and the churning of excitement in her stomach . "Extremely cute."

Marybeth lowered her voice. "Looks like you've got it bad, girl."

She quickly checked to see if Buck stood on Marybeth's other side.

"He's gone to get us each a drink. Am I right?"

Taking a quick breath, she nodded. "And if you can tell, so will the kids. They've never seen me like this. Nobody in this town has ever seen me like this. I want him so much I'm shaking."

Marybeth slid an arm around her waist. "Nothing wrong with that. It's about time you—"

"No. It's over the top, too much. I didn't expect—"

"I get that you're feeling a little vulnerable. That's only natural, but—"

"It's not just that. We promised each other we'd keep this on the downlow. I promised *myself* I wouldn't let him take up too much space, that I wouldn't—" She gulped as the song ended and Andy turned in her direction.

His gaze met hers with unerring accuracy. Carrying Mav back to the table where Beau and Jess sat, he headed straight for her.

Buck approached from the bar with their drinks. "Let's find a table and then— oh, hey, Andy. Any suggestions for where we should sit?"

"Beau and Jess saved three seats for you guys at our table."

"Terrific! Then we'll just follow you."

"Actually, I'd like to borrow Desiree for a dance, if you wouldn't mind taking her drink over there."

Marybeth gave her a quick squeeze and stepped away. "We'll do that. Go have fun."

"I'm sure we will." Andy held out his hand. "C'mon, Dez. Let's go show 'em how it's done."

"Sure thing." How she managed those two words was a mystery. When she slipped her hand into his, her pulse shifted into overdrive.

He led her to the dance floor as the band played the opening bars of *All I Want for Christmas Is You.*

"Perfect," he murmured, tucking her into his arms.

"Andy, I'm—"

"I know. I can tell. We'll work it out."

21

One glance at Desiree and Andy had hot-footed it over to ward off a full-blown panic attack. Holding her while they executed a snappy two-step seemed to help. She'd been rigid with fear in the beginning, but she'd softened up as they danced.

He looked into her eyes. "Talk to me, Dez."

"I'm turning into a nutcase."

"You? Never."

"That's what you think. That's what everyone thinks. I'm the one with a steady hand on the reins when it comes to my family, my career and my life. I can't go loony-tunes over... well... you."

He swallowed his first response of *Why the hell not?* Anyway, she'd told him. She had an image to uphold, that of a woman who had welcomed men into her life but didn't truly need any of them.

He'd thought commitment was the only minefield. Turned out her fears went much deeper. Loving him was fine. Needing him was something else entirely.

And she'd discovered while they'd been apart today that she needed him. Otherwise she wouldn't be freaking out. What should be cause for celebration had sent her into a tailspin.

How to play this? He took his best shot. "Not to minimize your reaction, but maybe I seem more special because you haven't been with someone for a while. Given time, you'll settle down."

"I doubt it."

He should be overjoyed that she expected this feeling to last. But she wasn't happy about it, which sucked. "Then how about this? We've enjoyed all the goodies of a relationship but not the minor irritations, like my dirty socks on the floor and my whiskers in the sink. Once you experience some of that, you'll—"

"Your socks were on the floor. I didn't care. And you wouldn't leave whiskers in the sink."

"Maybe not, but guaranteed you'll find things about me that are less than endearing. Before you know it, my halo will tarnish and you won't be loony-tunes anymore."

"I wish I could believe that."

"Believe it. This is temporary. We'll just get through it and then—"

"We? Are you feeling discombobulated, too?"

"Not anymore."

"What do you mean, not anymore?"

"I went through that phase after Mav was born. Grabbed any and every excuse to see you. But you acted like you just wanted to be friends, so the wild and crazy part settled into a subtle flow of wishful thinking."

"Aww." She glanced up at him. "I so want to kiss you right now."

The soft glow in her eyes quickened his breath. "Tough to do without causing a pileup on the dance floor. Want to head out to my truck for five or ten minutes?"

"Are you serious?"

He chuckled at her shocked expression. "Don't tell me you've never made out in a pickup, because I don't believe that for a minute."

"Of course I have! But that's for—"

"Kids? Honest to God, that's what I feel like. I can't wait to be alone with you."

"Same here, but we're not going out to your pickup."

"Why not? It'll be a long night. A make-out session in the truck might take the edge off until we can finally—"

"No. I'm not doing it. I refuse to give in to this... this...."

"Obsession for the hot guy you're dancing with?" He couldn't help himself. He had to gloat, just a little.

"Damn it, Andy, I missed you today. A lot."

"I missed you more."

"No, you didn't or you would have called me."

"I had the phone in my hand at least half-a-dozen times, maybe more."

"Why didn't you call?"

"Didn't want to be clingy. Why didn't you?"

"I couldn't come up with an excuse."

He held her gaze. "You don't need one. Ever. You can call me anytime, day or night."

Emotion flickered in those lovely hazel eyes. She likely knew what he was getting at. She'd clearly wanted to call because she'd missed him and needed to hear his voice. But without a plausible reason to disguise that need, she'd denied herself the call.

She took a breath. "You can call me anytime, too."

"Good to know." But he wouldn't consider it an open invitation. He'd be wise to ride herd on his neediness if she was putting a lock on hers.

* * *

He'd called it. Technically the longest night of the year had been the twenty-first, but in his view the twenty-fourth promised to take the prize.

From the moment the dance ended and he escorted Desiree back to the table, she gave him a wide berth. Physically they remained within sight of each other, but she focused all her attention on the babies — four-month-old Jodie and Susie, and newborn Elvira.

He pretended that Mav and Zach kept him so busy he didn't have time to ask for another dance. She didn't ask him, either, which was telling. Now that he was more accomplished, she'd taken to inviting him as often as he invited her. Not tonight.

Okay, so he'd eat his dinner, play with the kids and wait for the sleigh ride she'd promised to take with him later on. Should be fun.

The rides up and down Main Street kept the atmosphere in the Buffalo churning with the enthusiasm of returning riders and departing ones. Clearly it was the launch of a holiday tradition. Jess had snapped a bunch of pictures earlier that would appear in the New Year's edition of the *Sentinel*.

The McLintock siblings took turns driving the sleigh, so Mav and Zach made out like bandits, scoring extra rides right and left. The toddlers had recently become inseparable, so if one went, they both did.

That left Andy sitting at the table without a handy distraction. He could join Desiree in playing with the babies, but he had a hunch he'd get more points if he came up with something unexpected.

Excusing himself from the group gathered around their spot, he made his way over to the bar. Clint and Rance had their hands full keeping up with the orders and obviously the servers had fallen behind, too. Three trays of drinks stood waiting to be delivered.

Clint set another drink on the tray nearest him and glanced up. "Hey, Andy, what can I do for you?"

"I'd like to help pass out drinks."

"You would?" Clint blinked. "When you could be dancing with my mom?"

"I hate to interrupt her when she's having fun with those babies and it looks like you could use a hand."

"We could, but...." He shot a glance toward his mother's table as if to confirm she was otherwise occupied. "Okay, then. Thanks, Andy."

"Happy to be of service." Checking the number propped on the first tray in line, he hoisted it to his shoulder and headed for table five.

Nancy, Teresa and Annette, the Wenches besides Desiree who were single, grinned at his approach.

"What do we have here?" Teresa waved a hand at the tray. "They put you to work, did they?"

"Serving you three isn't work. When I saw where this tray was going, I begged them to let me deliver it."

"I'm not surprised." Nancy preened. "My gold outfit is a showstopper." She had a generous bosom and enjoyed dressing to highlight her assets.

"It's a stunner, all right." He passed out the steaming mugs of cider. "I don't remember seeing it before."

"It's new. For years I was stumped for Christmas outfits since yellow's not exactly a Christmas color, but gold works!"

"And I'm still stumped." Teresa, the only Wench who refused to color her gray hair, pointed to the Santa decorating her orange sweater. "His red suit and hat clash with the orange background, but whatcha gonna do?"

"You look great, Teresa. You, too, Annette." Her indigo sweater was the perfect backdrop for an intricate rendition of Santa and his reindeer flying through a moonlit night. The classy design suited her.

"Thanks." She looked pleased by the compliment. "I like it."

"Anything else I can bring you ladies?"

"Not unless you have any stray single men tucked away," Teresa said. "The supply's low since you're off the market."

He flushed.

"Aha!" Nancy crowed. "The rumor's true!"

"We're keeping it quiet."

Teresa laughed. "Good luck with that."

"Yeah, that may be an impossible dream. Anyway, holler if you want another round." Flashing them a smile, he made tracks for the bar.

Talk about déjà vu. High school all over again — first he'd invited Dez to a make-out session in his truck and he'd just been teased by her best friends. Heck, he was even waiting tables!

His teenage romances had all ended in heartbreak. He hadn't found the real deal until he'd met Mary. He'd wooed her with a gut-deep certainty that they were right for each other.

Desiree was the real deal, too, and he had the same gut-deep certainty. She was a challenge, though. Thank God he wasn't wet behind the ears this time around. That gave him a fighting chance.

He continued delivering drinks while enduring more teasing and veiled references to his relationship with Desiree. Clearly they were the talk of the town. So much for keeping it quiet.

He paused long enough to kiss the grandkids goodbye as their parents took them home. That deprived Desiree of her distraction of choice, but she didn't seek him out. Instead she stayed at the table talking with Buck and Marybeth.

Good thing she'd promised to take that sleigh ride with him. They needed to discuss the logistics of tonight's rendezvous. He'd be doing a lot of driving between now and the Christmas morning celebration at the ranch. He didn't care. The alternative was sleeping alone.

Ten minutes before their sleigh ride, he laughingly turned in his resignation to Clint, who refused to take it. He assigned him the lunch shift on Tuesday and gave him a raise.

Andy was still smiling about that as he approached the table. "Ready for a sleigh ride?"

"Absolutely." She stood without hesitation and took her coat off the back of her chair. "You looked like you were having fun delivering drinks."

"It was a blast." He glanced at Buck and Marybeth. "Did you folks schedule a sleigh ride?"

"Already took it," Marybeth said. "I've been in that sleigh many times out at the ranch, but sliding along Main Street is a whole other experience. I loved it."

"I'm sure I will, too." He helped Dez on with her coat and shrugged into his. He almost took her hand as they walked toward the entrance but changed his mind. Everyone might be talking about them, but that didn't mean she'd want him to confirm the suspicions.

Their driver was Desiree's adopted son Lucky, who stood beside the sleigh wearing his sheepskin coat, his Stetson, and earmuffs.

Dez peered at him. "Is it that cold going down the street that you need earmuffs?"

"No, ma'am, and I know they look dorky but I wore them so you two could have privacy to say anything you want."

That remark, uttered with sincerity and not a hint of a smirk, raised Andy's estimation of

Lucky considerably. He'd always liked the kid and they'd talked books endlessly whenever he visited L'Amour and More. But a twenty-something cowboy who'd wear dorky earmuffs in public as a kindness to his elders was a special sort of wonderful.

Andy held out his hand. "Thank you, son. I appreciate it."

"You're welcome." His grip was firm, his green eyes warm with emotion. "Normally I help the lady passengers in, but if you'd like to do it...."

"I would." He offered Desiree a hand up and felt the tension in her grip. Was that connected to passion or something else? He steadied her as she climbed in.

He followed and together they tucked the warm lap robe around their legs and feet.

"All set back there?" Lucky called out.

"We are, son," Desiree called back and Thor moved out, first at a walk and then at a brisk trot, his hoofbeats echoing off the buildings lining the street.

What an idyllic setting with the shops lit up with holiday decorations, the bells jingling in time with Thor's pace, and a few stray snowflakes drifting down from the opaque sky.

"Beautiful," Andy murmured, as he slid his fingers through hers under the lap robe.

"Yes." She hesitated. "Andy, I need..."

He held his breath and prayed that the next word would be the one he longed to hear.

"I need to take a little break, just to get my bearings."

He swallowed the soft curse word that threatened to spill out. "Okay. How long?"

"Just tonight and tomorrow night."

Could've been worse. "So you want me there on Tuesday night, when Steven's in residence?"

"Yes, please."

"Staying with you in your bedroom?"

"Yes."

"Just warning you, Dez, I won't be just window dressing. If I'm in your bed, I—"

"That's understood." Her voice trembled.

"Good." He held her hand for the rest of the ride, but they didn't speak again until he told her good night and she left the Buffalo with Marybeth and Buck.

It was gonna be one helluva Christmas.

22

Desiree changed her sheets and spritzed them with lavender. Hauling out her yoga mat, she spent thirty minutes stretching every muscle to work the kinks out.

Meanwhile, Sam paced near the back door, eager for his new best friend to show up.

"He's not coming, Sam. I told him not to, and he isn't the type to show up anyway. He respects my decision."

Was it the right one? Time would tell. Her first order of business was a good night's sleep. When she switched off the Christmas tree lights and crawled under the covers, Sam plopped down on his bed with a sigh of resignation.

She began with her tried and true sleep inducer, counting backwards from one hundred by threes. Nope. She replayed *McLintock*, scene-by-scene. Then she visualized favorite snatches of dialogue in every John Wayne movie ever made, including the duds.

Sometime after three in the morning she finally drifted off and was awake again before her alarm clock started glowing. Great. She'd be hollow-eyed and dull-witted for the biggest family holiday of the year.

But at least she'd killed the urge to jump Andy Hartmann's bones. That was a win. He could parade naked through her bedroom right now and she wouldn't care. Well, that wasn't exactly true.

She ached to see him, no matter what he was wearing or not wearing. No doubt he ached to see her, too. She'd handed him a big serving of Christmas disappointment and the look in his eyes haunted her, filling her with guilt.

Fear had outweighed guilt, though. She'd become fixated on him and that scared the stuffing out of her. Temporarily eliminating the sexual component was a first step in giving her some perspective.

She'd enjoyed the company of some amazing men but none of them had gotten under her skin like this except Charley. Her obsession with her first love made perfect sense, though. He'd changed her life and fathered a child who served as a constant reminder.

Andy hadn't changed her life... yet. She didn't want him to, either. But judging from how much she missed him when he wasn't around, he had the power to upset her personal applecart. Even now, when she felt like death warmed over and probably looked like it, too, she still longed to see him.

She wasn't worried that he'd take one look at her pitiful self and run in the other direction. He didn't care if her hair was a mess and she had bags under her eyes from lack of sleep.

Naturally he loved the outside of her because she was fun to have sex with, but he loved the inside of her, too, the part that made jokes and wrote books and admired sunsets.

No wonder she missed him like crazy. And it was a red flag, a warning sign of encroaching dependency.

Could she fix this glitch without abandoning the relationship? Could she learn to appreciate him when he was nearby and push him to the back of her mind when he wasn't? She'd mastered that with the other significant men in her life.

Her phone lit up with a text. *You awake?*

She misspelled *yes* twice before she got it right.

The phone rang and she answered so fast she almost dropped it. "I'm so sorry."

"It's okay."

"It's not. But I'm scared that I'll become dependent on you. I can't let that happen."

"I understand."

"Of course you do. You need a sweatshirt with *I understand* written on the front in big letters."

"Saying that I understand doesn't mean I don't want you lying under me right now, ready to come any second."

Lust slammed into her. "Is this a dirty phone call?"

"Seems to be going that way. Is it working for you?"

"Yes! It shouldn't be. Not after a miserable night that left me a wreck, but—"

"Can I stay tonight?"

"Might as well. My plan for dialing it back sucks."

He chuckled in that soft, intimate way that turned her insides to mush. "Sure does. See you in a couple hours. Love you, Dez." He disconnected before she could reply.

"You rat! Now I *really* miss you!" But she'd see him in two hours, along with her big, boisterous family. She and Andy would unveil Mav's new playhouse, the project that had jumpstarted their sexual connection.

She could look forward to an entire day with him, just like last Christmas. But unlike last year, he'd drive away with everyone else, then turn around and come back.

Adrenaline shot through her. She'd figure out the dependency thing later. Today she'd celebrate another magical Christmas with those she loved and end it in the arms of Andy Hartmann.

* * *

Knee-deep in wrapping paper, boxes and bows, Desiree sat in her traditional spot, the most comfortable easy chair in the living room, while she waited for the hubbub to die down. The playhouse would be the last gift of the morning.

Carols played in the background as Andy waded through the chaos to bring her a cup of coffee. "Thought you might be a quart low."

"Thanks. You're a lifesaver." Wrapping both hands around the mug, she took a sip. "Awesome."

He grabbed a footstool, pulled it over in front of her and perched on it. "How're you holding up?"

"Surprisingly well, but this will help. How about you?"

"I'm running on fumes. Might sneak back to one of the kids' rooms later and grab a quick nap."

"You didn't sleep, either?"

"Not much."

She lowered her voice. "They probably think we're tired because we wore each other out last night."

"If only."

"Thank you for the book. It's incredible that an autographed paperback is still in general circulation." She picked up the Louis L'Amour original from the pile of gifts next to her chair. "Where did you find it?"

"A used bookstore near the UM campus. I gave them more than they were asking. They didn't know what they had."

"And you bought it when?"

He smiled. "Last spring. Kept thinking I'd figure out a time to give it to you as the prelude to telling you I knew about M. R. Morrison."

"You're a patient man."

"Used to be."

"Used to be?"

"Friday night flipped a switch." His blue eyes took on a familiar gleam. "My patience is in short supply lately."

Her body clenched. "Stop looking at me like that."

"Then you stop looking at me like that."

She flushed. "Move a little so I can stand up. We need to do the thing."

"Here?" He scooted the footstool back and stood.

"You know what I mean. The Mav thing."

"Oh, *that* thing." He grinned and held out his hand. "C'mon, Grandma Dez. Showtime."

His grip was warm and familiar. She didn't want him to let go. But once she was upright, he turned her loose, following the rule they'd agreed on. No public displays of affection.

Walking over to where Mav sat on the floor, Andy crouched down.

She gave him a quick glance, then continued sorting through bows. She'd attached the sticky ones to her curly red hair, her clothes and the plush buffalo Clint and Tyra had given her.

"Hey, kiddo. You have another surprise coming."

She looked up, a red bow in her hand. Then she stuck it to the knee of his jeans.

"Why, thank you, Mav. That goes perfectly with my outfit."

She giggled and attached a green one to his other knee.

"And that one matches my shirt. Good job."

By now everyone had figured it was time for the playhouse and had drifted their way, including Zach. He had a death grip on a shiny red firetruck, his gift from Cheyenne and Kendall. He hunkered down next to Mav and she pasted a bow on his shirt.

Then she looked up, caught sight of the crowd and scrambled to her feet, clearly catching on that something was in the works.

Andy leaned toward her. "The surprise is in Rowdy Roost. Do you know the way there?"

Her face brightened and she pointed to the hallway leading out of the dining room.

"Excellent. Will you show us?"

She nodded and picked up the buffalo, clutching it to her chest as she started off.

Zach got ahead of her, but Molly pulled him back. "Hang on, son. Let her be in front."

When the little girl reached the swinging bar room doors, she dropped to her knees and crawled under them, dragging the buffalo with her. Zach was right behind her.

Andy made it in time to open the doors for Desiree, who had her hand on Sam's collar. She stepped through just as Mav got to her feet and stared at the playhouse.

"Look, Mav!" Zach started forward and Bret caught him by the shoulder.

"Hang on, sport."

Mav gazed at the playhouse, then glanced back, uncertainty in her green eyes.

"It's yours, sweetie." She kept a firm grip on Sam, who probably considered it his. "From Grandy and me. Your very own playhouse, just for you."

Mav switched her focus to Andy.

"All yours," he said. "Grandma Dez and I built it for you. You can go in."

That seemed to do the trick. With a squeal of excitement, she spun around, almost losing her balance. She righted herself and hurried toward the open door.

Zach wiggled with impatience. "Me, too, me, too."

"Remember it's hers." Bret let him go. "Ask if you can come in."

"Coming in!" he yelled out as he raced for the playhouse. Without waiting for permission, he dashed through the door and closed it behind him.

Andy threw up his arms. "And they're in!"

Everybody cheered. Then they took turns creeping over quietly and peering in the windows to see what the kids were doing.

"They're just sitting there looking pleased with themselves," Beau reported, laughing. "I'm sure I looked the same when I moved into my very own place."

"Let's go back in the living room." Desiree gave a soft command to Sam before starting toward the door. "I'm curious to find out what they'll do next."

It wasn't long before she had her answer. Turned out it was moving day. It took several trips, but eventually the toddlers transferred all their new toys from the living room to the playhouse.

Desiree followed in the beginning to monitor Sam, who wanted desperately to be part of the process. Then Zach took over the dog situation, letting Sam know with a raised hand and a firm command that he wasn't allowed in the playhouse. At the very end of the process, Zach navigated the hallway in the toy pickup she'd given him.

After giving them a little time to get settled, she beckoned to Andy. "Let's go take a peek."

He followed her down the hallway. Opening the swinging door slowly, she eased in.

The kids were inside the house having a conversation. Zach's actual words blended with Mav's babble, which had the cadence of real speech even if it made no sense. Maybe it made sense to Zach.

The little boy had parked his toddler-sized truck in front of the playhouse, exactly mimicking the way Bret parked his truck in front of the cabin he now shared with Molly and the kids. Zach and Mav's new stick horses sat outside, too, along with the buffalo and the miniature firetruck, even though the last two could fit in the house. Sam lay curled up near the door.

Andy smothered a laugh. "Clearly vehicles and animals belong outside," he murmured.

"Clearly."

He put his arm around her shoulders. "It's a hit."

"Yep." She pitched her voice low. "Am I to be called Grandma Dez, now?"

"Only if you like it. I opened my mouth and that came out."

"I do like it. For general use."

"I promise not to call you that in the bedroom."

"Good." She checked out the bows on his knees. "Gonna keep those on?"

"Definitely. It's my new look."

She gazed into his eyes, at peace with how things were, at least in this moment. "Merry Christmas, Grandy."

"Merry Christmas, Grandma Dez." He kissed her lightly on the mouth. "Let's go back to the party."

<u>*23*</u>

So far, so good. Andy was dead on his feet, but he was counting on a burst of energy that would turn him into a red-hot lover when he was finally alone with Dez.

Huge as the dining table was, it barely contained the crowd gathered around it. In a highly symbolic move, the McLintock kids insisted he should take one end of the table and their mom should take the other.

He'd rather they didn't do stuff like that, but evidently she thought it was funny. She even lobbed a dinner roll the length of the table when he asked if somebody would please pass him one. She had a good arm, a fact he'd discovered during a family baseball game this summer. She'd thrown him out at third.

As they finished dessert, Marybeth's pumpkin pie with whipped cream, the kids got fussy. Those without children stayed for kitchen duty while the four couples with offspring packed up.

Angie shooed him and Dez over to the entry along with Sam for the goodbye routine, setting another precedent. Again, Dez didn't seem to mind.

Beau and Jess were the last to go. Mav was resisting the idea of going home. She wasn't in tears yet, but she was close. She didn't want to leave her playhouse. "We'll come back for it tomorrow," Beau assured her for the umpteenth time.

"We'll keep it safe for you," Dez said, giving her a hug and a kiss.

Andy crouched down and met her serious gaze. "I promise it'll be right where you left it when you come back."

Patting his cheeks, she sniffled and gave a little nod.

"That's my brave girl."

She heaved a sigh. Then she pulled off the two bows still attached to his knees and smacked them against his chest, perfectly spaced, one for each nipple. They crinkled when he hugged her and kissed her on the cheek.

After they left, Dez gave him an amused glance. "That's borderline sexy."

"Should I keep them on?"

She laughed and moved closer. "No point. It'll all be coming off fast." Then footsteps headed for the hallway made her back off and change her tone. "Yeah, it would be great if you can be here in time to help get it on the flatbed."

"No worries. Just let me know when." Mention of the flatbed brought a wave of guilt. After Dez had left the Buffalo taking Buck and Marybeth with her, he'd made tracks for home, frustrated as hell. He should have stayed to help load the sleigh.

He wasn't a top hand like the McLintocks, but he should have at least offered to pitch in. Instead he'd slipped away to nurse his wounds.

Lucky walked into the entry holding Mav's buffalo. "Did Beau and Jess leave?"

"They did." Dez held out her hand for the stuffed animal. "I'll put it beside her playhouse. She's pretty tired so she might not miss it."

"Hope not. If they call, let me know. I'll drop it by their place on my way home."

"Thanks. Will do." Carrying the buffalo, she started toward the bustling kitchen, which provided a shortcut to Rowdy Roost. Then she turned back to him. "Feel free to gather up whatever's left on the dining room table."

"Yes, ma'am."

"I'll help," Andy said. "I vote we go the long way around and avoid the crowd. That's a zoo in there."

"Good plan."

As they walked down the hall, Andy grabbed the chance to apologize. "I should have stayed to help you guys get the sleigh on the flatbed last night. I honestly forgot about it."

Lucky blinked in surprise. "Thanks for the thought, but we didn't expect you to hang around for that."

"Maybe not, but I would have offered to lend a hand if I'd thought of it."

"After the publicity you gave us and all the tickets you bought, you deserved to sit back and enjoy yourself. Which I hope you did. With those earmuffs on I couldn't really tell if you had fun." He grinned. "But that was the idea, for me to be oblivious."

"It was an inspired idea. And we enjoyed the ride." A little white lie, one that was called for in this instance.

"I'm glad." As they walked through the deserted living room, Lucky glanced at the pile of gifts next to his mother's chair. "That was an awesome gift you found for Mom, by the way. I'm always on the lookout for autographed L'Amour books for her. I've only found one, and it had water stains. The one you gave her is in excellent condition."

"I was excited when I spotted it." He paused at the end of the dining table and began collecting dessert plates. "Anyway, I hope you had enough people to get that sucker loaded. Since the grandkids had to go home, you were down by four when I left. Clint and Rance were probably tied up with night owls at the Buffalo."

Lucky picked up empty coffee mugs. "They were, but we roped in Dallas this year, so we had him and Angie, plus Marsh, Ella, Gil and Faye. We made short work of it."

"Next year I'll stay, though. I wouldn't be surprised if we had more grandbabies by then. You could lose everyone you just named to the stork."

He laughed. "That is true. It's down to Rance and me, now. He'll go first. He's putting himself out there. I've never been good at that."

"It's not the only way you find the love of your life. Running your mom's bookstore puts you in an ideal spot to meet woman who love to read. That's a plus."

"Guess so." Then his brow puckered. "You said *the* love of your life. Does that mean you think there's only one?"

"I used to think that. I don't anymore."

His frown disappeared, replaced with a smile. "Right answer. You had me worried there for a minute."

"Hang on, son. I'm not saying—"

"I know, I know." Lucky came around the table and lowered his voice. "I realize you guys aren't committed to anything and we're all supposed to pretend we have no idea what's going on. But it's obvious to us that you're right for her and vice versa. We've compared notes and none of us have ever seen her like this."

His breath caught. "What do you mean, *like this*?"

"Completely, absolutely, bonkers. She'll get this goofy smile on her face whenever she looks at you, or even when she's thinking about you. She's taken to scanning the room to pinpoint your location. She was doing that last night at the Buffalo."

"She was? I thought she was ignoring me."

"Oh, no. The exact opposite. When your name comes up, she almost always blushes, which is kinda fun for us. Anyway, none of this is typical of her."

Andy managed to keep a grin from breaking through. "Maybe not recently, but it could've been true with some of the dads. When you're a kid, you don't necessarily notice such things." He didn't really believe that. Kids were often more perceptive than adults.

"When I say *we*, I'm including Buck and Marybeth. They've verified that this is new. They weren't around to witness how she reacted when Beau's dad was in the picture, but she didn't throw herself into his arms when he came back last year. It's safe to assume he's not the love of—"

"Hey, you two." The lady in question came down the hall from Rowdy Roost, her color high. "Are you licking those dessert plates clean or what?"

"Sorry, Dez." He picked up the last plate left on the table and turned toward her. Was that a goofy smile on her face? If so, it probably matched his. "I asked Lucky how things went with reloading the sleigh on the flatbed last night and we got to talking."

She glanced over his shoulder at Lucky. "Did you have a problem?"

"No, ma'am. But once we got on the topic, I couldn't seem to shut up about it."

"I can see why. The drama of loading objects on flatbeds is compelling subject matter."

Yep, she'd been eavesdropping. She'd likely caught the tail end of the conversation, if not all of it. He'd assumed she'd delivered the buffalo and made it back to the kitchen by the time they'd begun clearing the table.

But she'd lingered. Understandable. That playhouse had a bunch of memories attached to it. Since she'd heard at least some of the conversation, he might as well fess up. "We were talking about you."

"Uh-huh. Thought so."

"And it was my doing, not Lucky's."

"Not just your doing, Andy." Lucky faced his mother. "Sorry, Mom. I know I wasn't supposed to discuss this. It's just that Andy and I have been friends for quite a while. We connected even before Beau and Jess got together, so I—"

"I'm aware you have a connection with him, son. I've seen it. You two are book people." She included them both in an affectionate glance. "It creates a special bond. I totally understand the value of that. Now let's get those dishes in the kitchen."

He and Lucky gave her a *yes, ma'am* and followed her through the door. Lucky's comments touched him more than he'd let on. His visits to the bookstore had clearly meant a lot to the guy. They'd meant a lot to him, too.

Then it hit him. He hadn't just fallen in love with Dez. He'd fallen in love with the whole damn family.

24

After the kitchen was spotless and the living room put back in order, Desiree bid the rest of her family, and Andy, goodbye. Then she headed back to her bedroom, unbuttoning her shirt along the way, Sam prancing by her side.

Andy had taken him out earlier, as he'd announced to everyone, so he could save her the trouble. Ha. Somehow she'd met that comment with a polite *thank you* and a poker face. Goofy smiles? Really? Sheesh.

He'd continued to play the game well as they'd texted Jess and Beau to determine the best time to move the playhouse. The *Sentinel* office was closed on the twenty-sixth, so he and Jess had the day off to accomplish the task. They'd settled on ten o'clock.

He'd told everyone as they all were putting on their coats that he planned to get a good night's sleep so he'd be ready for the playhouse-moving gig. He'd suggested she do the same. No fair. She'd had to duck her head. Sure as the world she'd responded with a goofy smile to that one.

After Lucky's description of her behavior, she'd looked for those tells in Andy. He had them, but they were subtle — a hot glance that quickly cooled to a friendly gaze, a slight dent in his cheek that disappeared before it could bloom into a goofy smile. But then he'd had more time to practice disguising his feelings.

Obviously the gang had paid close attention to her the past couple of days, noticing things she wasn't even aware of. No question about it, she hadn't been herself since Friday night. To top it off, her temporary insanity had coincided with Christmas.

Trying to fix the issue on Christmas Eve had been a mistake. She wouldn't compound it by trying to find a solution tonight. But tomorrow she'd get a handle on this infatuation.

She had to. Day after tomorrow she'd be back at her desk working on the book she'd put aside a week ago. Although Steven would be staying at the house, he wouldn't be a distraction. He knew the rules when she was in writing mode.

She'd never discussed those rules with Andy. Hadn't seen the point. And yet she'd invited him to violate them by saying he could call her anytime.

Well, he could, but he wouldn't get through when she was writing. She had a list of the calls she would take if an emergency came up when she was working — currently her kids and Marybeth were the only ones on it.

Would that change? If she went by Sam's behavior, it would. When she came back from tossing her clothes in the hamper he stood by the almost invisible seam of the back door, ears pricked forward and tail wagging.

She could barely hear the rumble of Andy's truck and wasn't convinced she could distinguish it from the others. Not yet, anyway. But Sam could.

"You're a cupboard lover, Sam. Admit it. You're all about the doggie treats."

Sam spared her a brief glance, but his attention went right back to the door as the low growl of the truck's engine grew louder and stopped.

Her body quickened, her racing heart sending signals to her bare toes, to the tips of her fingers, to her mouth, to the moist entrance yearning for the pleasure this man could bring. She pulled Sam back from the door as it swung open and Andy came through it, hatless, his gaze hot.

Punching the button to close the door, he shoved the key fob in his coat pocket and pulled out a dog treat for Sam. Then he swept her into his arms. "God, it feels like years." His mouth came down on hers, hungry, demanding.

She fumbled with the buttons of his coat. He pulled at the tie of her robe, pushed aside the lapels and cradled her breasts. *Cold.* She gasped in shock.

He pulled back and let go. "Sorry, sorry. I just—"

"Come back here, you." Grabbing him by the coat collar, she tugged. "I don't care if your hands are cold. I want you. I want you *now*."

"Then now it is." Spinning her around, he pressed her against the wall.

"Wait. I didn't mean—"

"Hush. It'll be fun." He recaptured her mouth, his broad chest gently holding her in place.

His knuckles brushed her quivering stomach as he unfastened his belt, unfastened the button at his waist and unzipped his fly.

Were they really doing this? She hadn't tried this move since—

He eased his lips from hers as his belt clanked to the floor. His breathing was faster now. "When I pick you up—"

"I know." Her heart thundered as she gripped his shoulders through the thickness of his shearling coat. Then he lifted her, his hands were considerably warmer than before. She wrapped her legs around his hips.

He glanced down. One quick thrust and he was there. Panting, his voice rough and fire in his eyes, he met her gaze. "You okay?"

"You're crazy." And she was so turned on she couldn't see straight. She might come before he even got started.

"Crazy about you."

"You're still wearing your coat."

"The lady had a request." Dragging in air, he drew back. "So I—"

"You're showing off."

"And you like it." He pushed home and his breath hitched. "You *really* like it."

She gulped as another spasm hit. "When you're right, you're right. This'll be... quick."

"Don't hurry on my account." He pumped faster. "I could do this all day."

"Showoff, showoff, show—" She gasped as her body clenched. "There it is." She dug her fingers into the soft suede of his coat. "There. It. Ohhhhh." The climax roared through her at the same moment that he plunged in once more and came, swearing under his breath.

Then the swearing slowed and turned to a chuckle, which turned into laughter. His body shook with it until she got the giggles, too.

"Dez, look at us!" His grin took over his whole face. "Look at us having up-against-the-wall sex."

"Your idea, not mine."

"And you loved it, didn't you?" He squeezed her tush. "Didn't you?"

"Yes!" She looked into his beautiful blue eyes full of laughter. And love. "Sex with you is the best I've ever had."

The glow in his eyes grew more intense. "That's quite a compliment."

"I mean it. I feel like I just discovered what sex is all about."

He blinked. "Care to explain that?"

"I'll try. It's not about orgasms, although those are very nice. It's definitely not about beautiful bodies, although yours is lovely. It's not about performance, although you're awesome."

"Backatcha."

"It's about... fun. Yep, that's it. You even said it just now, when I started to object to doing it against the wall. You said *hush, it'll be fun.* And it was. And is, every time with you. It's your gift, Andy."

"Thank you." His voice was thick with emotion.

"Did I choke you up? I didn't mean to."

He cleared his throat. "Getting choked up isn't a bad thing." Leaning forward, he kissed her gently. "And now I'm going to put you down before I drop you. I doubt you'd find that fun."

"I doubt you would, either, considering we're still firmly linked. What's up with that?"

He slowly withdrew. "It seems my cock likes it so much in there it stays hard in hopes it won't have to leave."

She unwrapped her legs as he lowered her to the floor. "Don't let go, yet. I'm wobbly."

"That makes two of us." He surveyed the situation below his knees. "This has to be the most undignified post-coital position ever. I'm trapped in a potentially lethal combination of boots, jeans and undies."

"We'll work on it together. Let's start with your coat." She pushed it off his shoulders and let it fall. "Your shirt's soaked."

"I always wondered why more people don't have sex wearing a leather coat with a wool lining. Now I know." Unbuttoning his shirt, he peeled it off.

"Now we need to tackle your boots."

"You know, I've got this. If I can hold onto you for balance, I'll just toe 'em off and pull my feet out of the boots, the jeans and the briefs one at a time."

"Okay." She helped steady him as he extracted himself.

"Whew, that was a production. Before we try that again, remind me to take off more clothes."

"But that's what was so fun about it. You didn't stop for anything, not even to take off your coat. That's thrilling."

"Thrilling, huh?" He leaned against the wall and pulled off his socks. "I like the sound of that."

"And manly."

"I seem to remember you calling me a showoff." He picked up his clothes and laid them over the back of the easy chair.

"That's what's so great about what you did. You're not normally a showoff, so it's an exciting surprise when you act like that."

He smiled. "Glad you liked it. Ready to crawl into bed for some cuddle time?"

"Would you be horribly disappointed if I said I'd rather snuggle with you and go to sleep?"

"Would you be horribly disappointed if I said that's what I'd like, too?"

"Thank God." She let out a sigh of relief. "When you told everyone you were planning to get plenty of sleep tonight, I figured you meant the exact opposite. I put you through hell last night and I vowed to make up for it."

"Hey, you did. We won't come up with something that spectacular again tonight, especially when we're operating on two hours of sleep." He gestured toward the bed. "Go ahead and get in. I'll douse the Christmas tree lights."

"Thanks." Pulling back the covers, she climbed in on the left side, the one she'd claimed as hers. Although she'd become used to sleeping in the middle of the bed, it had taken her only one night to adapt to sharing it with Andy.

"Sam's out like a light, too." He turned off the Christmas tree.

"He was restless without you last night, too."

"Seriously? After I'd only slept here one night?" He got in on the other side and rolled toward her, pulling her close.

"I can't explain it, except you have a way about you that he really likes."

"It's the treats." He tucked her in close.

"It's more than that. He just likes having you around. So do I."

"Which worries you."

"It does." She stroked his chest and relaxed into his warmth. "But not tonight."

25

Andy left before dawn, had breakfast and showered at home, took care of a few chores and headed back out to Rowdy Ranch. He gave himself enough time to stop for gas.

Not that he cared, but he'd used a lot since Friday. Things would change after today, though. He'd only be making the round-trip at night for their rendezvous.

Meanwhile Steven would be hanging around Rowdy Ranch both day and night. The prospect didn't bother him the way it had five days ago, but if Steven was out at Rowdy Ranch and he was hard at work at the *Sentinel* in town, how was he supposed to befriend the guy?

Since it was Dez's idea, she likely had a plan. He just hadn't cared enough to ask. He would today, preferably before Grandpa #2 set foot on the property.

Beau's dark red F-350 sat in the parking area when he drove in. They must have arrived early since the clock on his dash read nine fifty-five. On impulse he drove around to the side door into Rowdy Roost.

Sure enough, the flatbed was already backed up to the barndoor look-alike. The door was partly open, as if folks had been going in and out to judge how best to load the playhouse.

But they hadn't done it yet. Good. He had a vested interest in that structure. He wanted to see it safely transferred.

He parked and got out, his boots crunching on old snow that remained in a shady patch. Voices drifted from inside — bursts of Mav's excited gibberish blended with adult conversation.

He sifted out Dez's comments from the rest. He'd learned to do that early, even before Mav was born. Her lilting tone was underscored by a hint of steel. Some people might miss it. Now that he knew her better, he never would.

"No worries. I think Andy just pulled up. I'll go check."

As he approached the opening, she appeared. "Ah, it is you."

"I saw they were here so I drove around."

"They were early. Mav's learned a version of the word *house.* It sounds more like *hus.* She's been repeating it endlessly ever since she woke up."

He laughed. "So they're eager to get this show on the road."

"Very eager. Sky came over to help. Since the truck bed tilts and we can drag the playhouse on the tarp, it shouldn't be hard, but I insisted we had to wait until you arrived."

"I appreciate that. I'm no expert at this, but since we're the ones who put it together—"

"We both need to be there when it gets moved. That's what I told them. They understand."

"I'm not surprised they're early. I should have followed my instincts and done the same. Anyway, let's go do this." He stepped toward her.

"One more thing."

He paused.

"Steven will be here between eleven-thirty and twelve. I told him to come to Beau's house, since we'd be over there getting this set up on their back porch. Beau and Jess offered to feed us all lunch."

"*All* of us?"

"Yes. They want you there to set the tone."

"Which is?"

"That you're the grandfather who's been here from the get-go, the one they've been able to count on. He doesn't get to sweep in and try to minimize your contribution to the family with elaborate gifts and grandiose promises."

"I see. You must have told them about your phone conversation with him."

"I did. They weren't impressed. Are you up for that? You don't have to, but—"

"I wouldn't miss it. Should be an interesting lunch."

* * *

The playhouse loaded like a dream. Nothing fell off or came apart. Sky drove the flatbed, Beau, Jess and Mav followed in their truck, and Andy gave Dez a ride over in his.

Sky backed the truck right up to the porch steps. Beau had measured the height of the porch and the height of the flatbed. The porch was two inches above the lip of the truck bed.

Andy stood beside the porch holding Mav so she could watch the proceedings and Dez tucked in beside him. Nobody said a word as Sky and Beau eased the playhouse over the lip of the porch. When it was off the truck and on the porch, everyone cheered.

In the spot where the playhouse would sit, Jess had spread a colorful oilcloth on the porch floor and anchored it with bricks. Sliding it off the tarp and onto the oilcloth took no time at all.

Mav wiggled to get down and Jess opened the playhouse door. Chanting *hus, hus, hus,* she hurried inside and pulled the door shut.

Beau laughed. "And that's the last they ever saw of Maverick McLintock."

Arms wide, Jess came over to wrap Andy and Dez in a group hug. "You guys are the best. Thank you."

"It was a fun project." He said it without thinking about how it could apply to building the playhouse and... everything that had happened as a result. Oh, well.

Jess grinned. "I'm glad it was."

"It had better be a fun project." Beau came over with the folded tarp. Sky just told me he'll pour a foundation for Susie's this summer. That way they won't have to mess with this porch routine."

"I said I *might* do that." Sky sauntered over, his hat tipped back. "Depending on whether Mom and Andy can see themselves building another one.

And I'm willing to help, unlike my lazy little brother, here."

"I was willing to help! Jess told me I couldn't. Back me up, here, Jess."

"I could tell they wanted to do it themselves. It's more meaningful that way, right, guys?"

Dez smiled. "It was. I'm even thinking of ordering a little plaque to hang on it — *Built with Love by Grandy and Grandma Dez.*"

"So it's official?" Beau glanced at her.

"W-what do you mean, *official*?"

"That we're calling you Grandma Dez."

"Oh! I guess so. Andy came up with it, although he's the only one who calls me Dez."

Beau put his arm around her shoulders and gave her a squeeze. "You look like a Grandma Dez. I like it. Good job, Andy."

"What do you mean, *I look like a—*"

"You know — spunky, ready for anything, cool."

Sky nodded. "She does look like a Grandma Dez. I like it, too."

"That makes three of us." Jess glanced at Sky. "Are you sure you can't stay for lunch? Beau made Marybeth's chicken soup."

"Did he now?" Sky's eyebrows shot up. "I don't think I understood the importance of this lunch."

"My dad caught me unprepared last year, but I'm ready for him this time. We're gonna bypass the artificial crap and get real."

"Now I really wish I could stay. But the flatbed has to be returned today and I promised

Penny we'd take Susie for a short ride this afternoon since the sun's out today. I need to make tracks. Keep me informed, bro. I've got your back."

"Yeah, but do you have my front? That's where the kill shot comes from in the movies. I—"

"Good luck, everyone." Sky tipped his hat. "Enjoy that soup."

As he drove away, Jess looked over at Andy. "Did Desiree tell you about the soup?"

"She did. Good choice."

"And here comes our guest now." Dez shaded her eyes. "Or not. I've never known Steven to drive a truck, let alone a dually."

Beau let out a low whistle. "Whoever that is got themselves a sweet ride. I'll chose red every time, but that metallic gray has it goin' on. I didn't know you could rent a dually."

"I'm not sure you can." Andy glanced at Dez. "Did he say how long he was staying?"

"I can't remember. Probably just a few days. Why?"

"Because if that's him, I'm guessing he bought himself a big ol' truck."

"That's ridiculous. It can't be him."

Andy pulled out his phone. "Timing's right. Beau, are you expecting anybody else?"

"No, sir. Not only that, I can't think of anybody around here who drives a metallic gray F-350, let alone one with dual tires. That thing's brand new. Looks like it just came off the showroom floor."

The low-throated rumble of the powerful engine canceled any more attempts at conversation as it pulled in and parked beside Andy's truck, dwarfing it. The light was such that he couldn't get a good look at the driver, but it didn't matter.

It was Steven. Had to be. Dez had nailed his intentions — to win her back and live out his golden years on Rowdy Ranch. Despite what she'd told him on the phone, he planned to roll right over the competition in that ginormous rig.

Good thing the woman standing next to him had no use for this kind of display. Steven didn't know her very well if he thought it was the way to her heart.

Then again, the way to her heart was still blurry for him, and he knew her pretty damn well. It definitely didn't involve driving up in a huge and massively expensive truck, though. Beyond that, he was still guessing.

26

Desiree almost felt sorry for the man who'd agreed to father her second child. Had he been this dense when they'd met? Had she been blind to his belief that money could buy love?

He was clearly bewildered by the family tradition of serving chicken soup to create an atmosphere of trust. He enjoyed eating it and seemed a little less manic after he'd had a couple of bowls, but he didn't understand… anything.

On some level he might sense he was a psychological mess and that his salvation lay in returning to the only family he had. But she wasn't going to take him in and rehabilitate him.

It wasn't up to Beau and Jess, either. Or Andy. When Beau offered to take Steven out to see Slim and Pickens, his pot-bellied pigs, Mav went along. Desiree stayed behind with Jess and Andy, saying she'd help with cleanup.

Instead she asked them both to sit back down. "Listen, Andy, forget that I asked you to be his friend and guide him in the ways of being a father and grandfather. I didn't understand the scope of his issues."

"Hey, I'm still willing to—"

"No, seriously, he could be such a time suck. And he might hang around a long time, hoping he can manufacture a reason to stay."

"Like talking you into getting back with him."

"That's Plan A. He's a trained salesman and he's convinced he can sell me on the idea."

"Then I'd be happy to set him straight on that score."

Jess laughed. "I'm sure you would, Dad."

"I'll handle him, Andy. He's my responsibility more than anyone's. I'm the one who—"

"But if you hadn't hooked up with him," Jess said, "we wouldn't have Beau. I'm so grateful to you that Beau exists, and to Steven, when it comes to that. I'm more than willing to do whatever—"

"That's another thing I'm afraid of, that you and Beau will allow yourselves to be saddled with him. It would be great if you could have a normal relationship, but at this point I don't think he's capable of that. He could drive you crazy."

"She has a point," Andy said. "You have Mav to consider. I should be the one to take the brunt of the—"

"Nobody should have to be the one. He's turned into a rich, clueless man who has no idea how to relate to people without buying them stuff."

"That's obvious." Jess sighed. "I was relieved when he didn't come in loaded down with gifts, but taking us shopping in Missoula sounds even worse. Mav's too young to handle that and for Beau and me it would be like our daddy buying us treats. We'd hate it."

Andy leaned back in his chair, his expression thoughtful. "So what's your plan, Dez?"

"I don't have one, damn it. I'll come up with one, but in the meantime, please don't indulge this guy and make yourselves miserable in the process. You're both kind-hearted and I cherish that, but Steven is a load neither of you need to carry. And that goes for Beau, too."

"You're not obligated to carry it either, Dez." Andy held her gaze. "You say he's your responsibility, but I disagree. Building on what Jess said, we owe you one. Because of Steven we have Beau. And because of Beau, and some help from Jess's cat, we have that little munchkin who lights up all our lives. We have Mav."

Jess gave a whoop. "Well said, Dad! I declare you the winner in this debate. What say you, Grandma Dez?"

She let out a breath. "I say I'm a lucky lady to have you guys. Okay, we'll tag-team this deal and take it in shifts. Andy, you should probably go home. You bring out the braggart in him."

"Doesn't take much," he muttered. "But if I leave, how will you—"

"I'll ride back to the house with him. This afternoon will be my shift."

He grimaced.

"It's the logical thing to do. Maybe I can talk some sense into him."

"Could you please let him know that we appreciate the thought behind the shopping trip, but it would be..." Jess paused.

"A nightmare?"

"Yes, but don't say that. How about *logistically impractical.*"

"That works. He'll want to get you all Christmas presents, though, the more extravagant the better."

"Promise him I'll come up with ideas, preferably ones that don't involve shopping. Beau and I have talked about taking a road trip to Apple Grove with Mav next spring and staying at that beautiful old hotel."

"I'll mention that. Did I tell you I'm putting him in Beau's old room?"

"Oh, my goodness. I keep telling Beau we need to come over and clean out all the souvenirs his dad—"

"I'm glad you didn't get around to it. Marybeth and I decided we wouldn't even dust those shelves. Maybe he'll get the point that — I hear footsteps on the back porch. C'mon, Andy. Let's get our coats. I'll walk you out to your truck."

"Okay." He sighed in resignation and followed her into the living room. "You know I hate this, right?" He helped her on with her coat and shrugged into his before grabbing his hat.

"I'm not happy about it, either. Was he this bad when he visited last year?"

He opened the door for her. "If you mean did he act like he was all that and a bag of chips, yes." Following her out, he closed the door, blocking the sound of Steven's voice in the kitchen.

"I guess I was so focused on Mav at the time I didn't pay much attention to him."

Crossing the porch, he took her hand as they went down the steps. "He was slightly less annoying and way more disoriented on that trip, maybe because he didn't have a plan. Now he has one and thinks it's brilliant."

"Don't worry. I'll torpedo that fantasy."

"I'll bet you a bottle of your favorite wine he has a ring in his pocket."

"No!" She stopped in her tracks and stared at him. "What kind of idiot would show up with a ring after I told him I was involved with someone else?"

"You said you were sleeping with me. You didn't say we were engaged. Therefore he still has an opening, at least in his mind."

She came closer. "Well, he's sadly mistaken."

"I know." His chest heaved. "I told myself I was fine with him being at the house with you when I'm not around, but now that he's actually here and it's obvious what he's up to, I just...."

"He has nothing to give me, Andy." She cupped his jaw and moved in, brushing her mouth over his. Then she stepped back. "I'll see you tonight."

"What time? Will you have dinner with him? What if he—"

"I should have mentioned that Marybeth's part of this tag-team idea. She's been busy making and freezing soup, stew and chili in single-serving containers. I plan to eat in my room and let Steven fend for himself."

"That's good news."

"How does eight sound?"

He opened his mouth, closed it again.

"What?"

"Nothing. Eight sounds perfect. See you then." He gave her a quick, firm kiss and headed for his truck.

As she watched him drive away, the hinges of the front door creaked behind her. "There you are."

She turned as Steven clattered down the porch steps wearing his shearling coat and a Stetson with bling on the hatband. He looked like a model for Western wear.

Beau took after him, which meant Beau would age well, too. When choosing potential fathers for her children, she'd factored in appearance and Steven was a handsome man. He didn't inspire the slightest flutter in her stomach.

"Beau and Jess put Mav down for a nap." He sauntered toward her, smiling. "So I figured we might as well head home."

Home. He'd likely chosen the word on purpose and it sandpapered her already frazzled nerves. But it was her shift and the sooner she told him the way things were, the better. "Sounds like a plan."

"Then let's go." He reached for her arm but she stepped sideways and walked quickly to the passenger side of his truck.

He lengthened his stride, opened the door and attempted to help her in.

"Thanks, I've got it."

He chuckled. "Still got that independent streak, I see." He closed the door.

The interior smelled brand new. Once upon a time she'd enjoyed that smell because it signified that she had enough money to buy a new truck when she needed it. These days she preferred the familiar scents of woodsmoke and horses.

"What do you think of my new ride?" He slid behind the wheel, closed his door and buckled up.

"It's big."

"Yes, ma'am." He switched on the motor. "Love that sound. This baby's got power."

"So I see. What do you plan to do with this truck?"

"Whatever I want. That's why I got this one. It can do it all — pull a horse trailer or an RV, go off-road, haul hay, building supplies, whatever." He checked his mirrors several times as he put it in reverse and slowly backed out, his jaw tight.

She crossed her fingers he wouldn't hit anything. Beau valued the trees in his yard. She didn't relax until he was pointed in the right direction.

"You're welcome to drive it any time you want."

"Thanks, but I'm all set in that department."

"As I recall you have a purple one."

"I do."

"Does it have the dual wheels on the back?"

"No."

"See, there might be a time you need extra hauling power, in which case, you can make use of this one."

She turned to him. "Steven, what are you doing here?"

"I thought it was obvious. I wanted to celebrate Christmas with you. Well, you and the kids. And the grandkid. I'm still not sure why you didn't want me to come until today, but your house, your rules."

"How long are you planning to stay?"

"As long as you'll have me."

"What?"

"Desiree, we're at a point in our lives when it's time to settle down, forget the daily grind and enjoy life. I'm sure that's why you've taken up with Andy Hartmann. And he's okay, but you don't have a lot to choose from in Wagon Train."

She stared at him in shock. "You think I *settled* for Andy?"

"Of course. Be honest. You could buy and sell the guy. He's—"

"Twice the man you are! No, I take that back. He's three or four times the man you are!"

He glanced at her in confusion. "Don't tell me you're in love with him."

"Yes, I am." She quivered with rage. "And I'll thank you not to say anything disparaging about him in my presence ever again."

"Hey, I'm sorry. You just said you were sleeping with him. You didn't mention any kind of commitment or love connection. Has he asked you to marry him?"

"That's none of your business."

"Which means he hasn't." He glanced out the window. "Did I miss the turn? I think I missed the turn." He pulled to the side of the road and put on the brakes.

She checked their surroundings. In the heat of the moment, she'd lost track of where they were. "Yes, you missed the turn. You'll have to swing around and go back. Or even better, you can let me out here and drive back to town. Now that Christmas is over, the hotel probably has rooms available."

"You don't want me to stay with you?"

Dear Lord, he looked like a little boy who'd just had his favorite toy snatched away. Her anger slowly evaporated. "Steven, I don't know what kind of scenario you've created in your head, but—"

"It's the only scenario that makes sense. It brings everything full circle." Reaching in his pocket, he pulled out a ring box.

"Oh, no. Steven, don't do this. Don't—"

"Desiree Annabelle McLintock, will you marry me?" He snapped open the velvet box to reveal a diamond the size of one of Marybeth's cheese puffs.

She had to be having a nightmare. The first proposal of her life wouldn't take place in the cab of a truck by the side of the road. And it wouldn't come from a man she hardly knew anymore. "I can't believe you bought me a ring."

"I can't believe it's taken me this long to give you one. I bought you a ring right after you told me you were pregnant."

"You did?" She looked up, then dropped her gaze. She couldn't bear the hopeful light in his eyes.

"I carried it around for weeks while I debated whether I should ask you and try to make a life with you and our baby. By then you'd found out we'd have a boy. Everything I read told me that I was in danger of treating him the way my father had treated me. In the end I lost my nerve and returned the ring."

Should she tell him she wouldn't have accepted his proposal? And was she absolutely sure that was true? No. She took a ragged breath and gathered her courage.

She looked him straight in the eye. "That's a beautiful ring."

"It'll fit, too. I kept the little card where I'd written down the size."

"I can't marry you. I'm in love with Andy."

"But he hasn't asked you to marry him. That's what I'm offering. When I left I expected you to end up marrying someone else, but you didn't. That was my fault. I hurt you by leaving and you never got over that."

The poor man. She was going to destroy his lovely fantasy but it couldn't be helped. "You're not the reason I've never married. The reasons are complicated but they have nothing to do with you. Andy would marry me in a minute if I agreed. He hasn't proposed because I told him not to."

He frowned. "That's nuts. You just admitted you're in love with him. Why wouldn't you—"

"Like I said, it's complicated. But the bottom line is that I won't marry you. Ever."

"I don't believe you."

"You don't have to, but you do have to promise not to bring up the subject."

"Do you still want me to go to the hotel?"

She let out a breath. "You can stay at the house, but only if you make that promise."

"Sure, okay. I promise. But I'm guessing when you have a chance to think about it, you'll change your mind."

"I won't, and if you make any reference to it whatsoever, you're out."

"Understood."

27

The rest of the day dragged. Andy made himself something for dinner that he barely tasted. Then, since he had the time, he showered, shaved and dressed in clean clothes.

How long would this evening schedule continue? He wasn't about to ask when it was less than a week old, but he was curious if Dez would ever want a different arrangement. The ball was in her court on that, though.

The road was deserted and he ignored the speed limit. Consequently he arrived fifteen minutes early. Couldn't very well sit out there and wait until the appointed time when Sam would be prancing around the doorway.

The aroma of a cedar fire tickled his nose as he swung down from the driver's seat and closed the door. The lady enjoyed atmosphere. So did he. Every time he pushed the button on the key fob he felt like a character in a movie — the hero, of course.

Doggie treat in one hand and key fob in the other, he activated the mechanism. The door swung open to reveal Dez propped up in bed reading a book, a small blaze in the beehive fireplace casting a warm glow over her bare breasts, and Sam sitting smack dab in front of him with a grin on his doggie face.

"I guess somebody decided she was over the sex-against-the-wall routine."

"Not necessarily. I thought we could start slow and build up to it." She set aside the book. "You're early."

"I had a bad case of lead foot." He gave Sam his treat and clicked the button to close the door. "Whatcha reading?"

"The Kama Sutra."

"Really?"

"No, not really. I'm reading the one you gave me for Christmas. I've read it before, but it sounds better autographed."

"I agree." He took off his coat, left it over the back of the easy chair and toed off his boots. "I read it again, too. Pretended I could hear his voice narrating the story." He stripped off his shirt.

"I'm doing that, too! It's not such a stretch. He held this very book in his hand while he autographed it." Her gaze lingered on his chest. "You look good in firelight."

"So do you." He tossed his shirt on the chair and unbuckled his belt. "Was I right about the ring?"

She groaned. "Yeeesss. And boy, was it a rock. He thinks he broke my heart and that's why I never married. So now he wants to do the right thing."

"And you said...." He paused, his fingers on the metal button at his waist, his chest tighter than it should be.

"That I couldn't accept his proposal because I'm in love with you."

He let out a breath and unzipped his jeans. "How'd he take that?"

"He was confused, especially after I told him you were willing to propose but I asked you not to."

"I imagine that threw him for a loop." He was confused about it, too, but that was a whole other discussion. "Then is he returning the truck and going back wherever he came from with his tail between his legs?"

"Los Angeles, and no, he's not leaving yet. He's convinced when I have a chance to think about it, I'll change my mind."

Getting rid of his jeans and briefs, he walked over to the bed. "Are you thinking about it?"

"No." She threw back the covers and wiggled down so she was flat on her back. "I'm thinking about what you're thinking about."

"You can read my mind?"

"It's not hard." She stared at his johnson.

"Then you need glasses."

"Very funny. Time to get busy, Hartmann." She opened her arms and spread her thighs.

He nearly came just looking at her. "Then I guess you don't want to hear my idea about how to deal with Steven."

"Not now."

"Good, because I can't remember what it is anymore." Climbing into the sweet-smelling bed, he moved between her thighs, leaned down and kissed the living daylights out of her. Postponing the moment gave him a chance to rein in his lust.

Eventually she took hold of his cock and he had no choice but to go where she indicated he should. Sinking into her rivaled every other sensual experience he could think of.

Then he stopped thinking altogether as his instincts took over. Tuned in to every moan, every ripple, every hitch in her breathing, he loved her gently at first, then harder, then with everything in him until she let go. He rode the waves of her climax to his own, pounding into her slick channel, out of his mind, saturated with pleasure.

When it was over, he lowered his chest until it rested lightly against her nipples because he knew she liked that. He nuzzled a tender spot behind her ear because he knew she liked that, too.

She kneaded his glutes because he'd told her that felt good. And she wrapped her silky legs around his hairy ones because that pleased both of them.

He sighed. "I love making love to you."

"I can tell. I feel fully loved. I hope you do, too."

"I feel so fully loved I almost can't hold it all."

"We don't need the *Kama Sutra*."

"Not yet, anyway. I suppose we could get bored."

"You think so?"

"No."

"Me, either. I wonder if anyone's ever had their muscles lock up when they're in the middle of a complicated position."

"Odds are they have. But it could happen in the good-old missionary position, too."

"It could, but not as likely. Everybody rags on the missionary position but it's my favorite."

"Because of chest hair."

"Because of chest hair, and because we can kiss this way, and I can see your face."

Lifting his head, he gazed into her eyes. "I like that part, too. But then I like everything about being naked with you."

"Ditto." She held his gaze. "But I think by talking about muscle cramps I just got one."

"Uh-oh. Where?"

"My left calf."

"Let me work on it." Easing away from her, he moved to her left side, sat near her calf and slowly massaged it. "Does that help."

"A little. It's starting to go away. Tell me your idea."

"About what?"

"Steven."

"Oh. I say we sic the Wenches on him."

She grinned. "I like it already. What do you have in mind?"

"When I was delivering drinks on Christmas Eve, Teresa was bemoaning the lack of single men. Well, now we've got one."

"Steven? I wouldn't wish him on anyone, let alone one of them."

"I get that, but what if he's redeemable?"

"Naturally I want to think he is for Beau's sake. And Mav's. But it'll be a lot of work. Even if I wanted to take on the job, he'd take my involvement as evidence that I still long for him."

"Would he go to therapy?"

"Not unless he thought doing it would convince me to take him back. He's stuck on the idea that we belong together."

"Because he doesn't see an alternative. I'm not suggesting any of the Wenches marry the guy, but what if one of them asked him out?"

"Assuming he'd go, he'd likely spend the evening bragging about his truck and the size of his bank account. They don't care about his bottom line."

"And that's something he needs to learn. Would one of them have fun rehabilitating him?"

She hesitated. "Maybe. Teresa's right. There aren't a lot of single guys our age in Wagon Train."

"Can he dance?"

"Yes. That I remember."

"That's a plus. Much as I hate to admit it, he's a handsome bastard. Is he good in bed?"

"How do I know?"

"Okay, *was* he good in bed?"

"Not as good as you."

"*I* wasn't as good as me when I was… how old was he then?"

"Twenty-eight."

"Yeah, I was still learning back then. Still am."

She chuckled. "Feel free to practice on me."

"Every time, Dez. It's an adventure." He kneaded the muscle in her calf. "How's your leg?"

"Wonderful. You have magic fingers."

"Maybe I should do your foot, too, just to be sure it doesn't come back."

"You can do any part of me you want."

"I'll keep that in mind." Propping her foot in his lap, he worked his thumb up the arch from her heel to her toes.

She groaned with pleasure. "Where have you been all my life?"

"Right here, waiting for a playhouse to arrive." But her light-hearted comment resonated. No doubt she'd been searching for something, for someone, for years. Would she wake up and see that she'd found it in this amazing connection they had?

But the subject of the moment was Steven, a guy who needed to change his focus. Although he wasn't a threat, he was an unwelcome distraction. "Okay, we don't know if Steven can deliver in the bedroom, but he's probably had plenty of experience. Let's hope he learned a thing or two."

"I don't remember him being a selfish lover. If he had been, he would have been gone after the first night, even if he could give me beautiful babies." She let out a happy sigh. "You're going to be sorry you started this foot massage. I never want you to stop."

"Think I'd fit under your desk while you're typing?"

"Oh, man, that would be a writer's dream. Think of all the extra words I'd get."

"Are you back at it tomorrow?"

"I am. Which reminds me, I said you could call anytime, but when I'm writing, I usually don't answer—"

"Which won't be an issue if I'm under your desk massaging your feet."

"True, but then the *Sentinel* would lose its talented editorial writer. I'll forego the foot rub for the good of the town."

"Noble of you. And don't worry about me calling or texting when you're writing. I didn't before and just because our relationship has changed doesn't mean that has, especially now that Christmas is over."

"Mostly. When I say I'm getting back to the book, it's just so I don't go two weeks without touching it. I'll break for New Year's. But on January second, it's pedal to the metal."

"Think you might have time to call a meeting of the Wenches this week to broach the topic of Steven?"

"I'll make time. I'll see if everyone's free tomorrow night. In fact, if they are, I'll make sure he's on hand. I'll tell him we need a private business meeting, but after that I'd like him to come and meet everyone. He didn't get the chance last year."

"He'll be the center of attention in a room full of women. He'll love that. Well, unless you skewer him. That isn't what I—"

"Oh, don't worry, we won't. That would defeat the purpose. We want him to be open to change, which requires a light touch, not a sledgehammer."

"This might work, Dez."

"Let's hope it does. Are you finished doing my foot?"

"I can be."

"Good. Then please do me."

28

All the Wenches said yes to a meeting that would begin at seven. Jess couldn't stop laughing when Desiree called to tell her the plan, especially when she found out it was her dad's idea.

Marybeth loved the concept and offered to make snacks. Desiree decided to go a little fancy and made a big kettle of mulled wine using the oranges left over from the ones she'd bought for the grandkids' stockings.

She'd spent the day writing and to her surprise, the words flowed easily. Often after a few days off she had trouble getting into the story, but not this time.

Whenever she'd taken a break to get a fresh cup of coffee, she'd pictured Andy in his office at the *Sentinel*, typing away on his New Year's editorial. She always looked forward to that one. He never failed to make her smile or give her something to think about.

Beau had cleared his calendar between Christmas and New Year's so he could spend time with his dad, so Steven had been gone the whole day and was eating dinner over at Beau's too. But he'd promised to be back by seven-thirty so he could meet the Wenches.

They hadn't existed during the time they'd been together and he'd been touchingly pleased that she wanted to introduce him to the group. Such moments of humility renewed her hope that he might eventually become a guy Beau could admire.

When he'd visited last year and stayed in town, he'd only been in her house briefly and she hadn't been comfortable with showing him around. She still didn't plan to give him a tour or tell him about the secret back door to her bedroom.

But she'd finally had to show him the revolving bookcase or leave him to think she could walk through walls. He'd been fascinated with it, as nearly everyone was. She'd emphasized that he was not to use it, though. He could text her if he had an urgent problem.

The Wenches arrived on time as usual, talking and laughing as they met in the parking area and tromped up the steps to the front door. Sam happily greeted each one as they milled around in the kitchen serving themselves mulled wine and loading small plates with goodies set out by Marybeth.

The collie followed them to the library and stood outside looking hopeful as they filed in.

"Sorry, sweetie." Desiree gave him a treat. "Go lie down. We're going to have a meeting."

With great reluctance, he walked to his bed in the living room and she closed the library door. She'd tried letting him in, but when snacks were involved, certain Wenches couldn't resist feeding her dog.

Since Jess had as much or more at stake in this venture, Desiree had decided she should wear the tiara, hold the scepter and occupy the place of honor. She'd placed Jess's green wingback facing the semicircle of the other six rainbow chairs.

That put Nancy to Jess's left in the yellow chair, followed by Teresa in orange, Colleen in red, herself in violet, Annette in indigo and Cindy in blue on Jess's right. Steven's chair would be brought in later.

Green eyes sparkling, Jess raised the scepter. "I hereby call to order an official meeting of the Wenches Who Read in the name of Louis L'Amour. "

Everyone chanted *hear, hear* and lifted their glasses of mulled wine.

"First order of business, my father-n-law, Steven Jacobson. Here's my thumbnail sketch. Steven is gorgeous, an older version of Beau, graying at the temples, beautiful brown eyes, around six-two and fit. Oh, and he's single."

"Sounds yummy," Nancy said. "Can't wait to meet him."

"But there's a catch," Jess continued.

Teresa sighed. "Isn't there always? Is he a jerk? A felon? A psycho?"

"None of the above. He's a bit... insecure."

Nancy waved a hand. "Aren't we all?"

"Not me." Cindy fluffed her short hair, dyed red and green for the season. "I'm comfortable in my own skin. And my hair color."

"Why do you say he's insecure, Jess?" Annette asked.

"He tries to impress people with his money and possessions."

"Alrighty then. That's good info." Teresa beamed at her. "Let's hit him up for a big contribution to the Firehouse Fund. We'll let him know we're all impressed as hell."

Jess nodded. "Good idea. I didn't think of it. If he's throwing money around, he might as well support a good cause."

"How do you know he's throwing money around?" Nancy bit into one of Marybeth's cheese puffs.

"His truck, for one thing. He's over at my house with Beau and Mav, and he'll be driving back here shortly in his brand-new F-350 dually."

"Whoa." Teresa's eyes widened. "Does he have a ranch or what?"

"He does not. The truck is a status symbol to impress all of us, but mostly Grandma Dez."

Colleen laughed and turned to Desiree. "Cute! Is that gonna be your granny name?"

She smiled. "Looks like it."

"Well, I approve. Anyway, continue, Jess. Tell us more. Can he dance? Play the harmonica?"

"The harmonica?" Annette shot her a look. "Where'd that come from?"

"Harmonica players are good kissers."

"Are you telling me that George—"

"Yes, and yes."

"I don't know if he plays the harmonica," Jess said, "but according to Desiree, he can dance."

"Which means he has rhythm." Cindy executed a shimmy. "Rhythm is *so* important, if you get my drift."

Teresa grinned. "Preach it, sister."

"Just to be clear, I checked with Desiree on this point and she's making no promises. He was okay thirty-some years ago, but—"

"Just okay?" Colleen swiveled in her chair. "C'mon, Desiree, that's not much of an endorsement."

"All right. He was better than okay. Happy, now?"

"I am," Nancy said. "When Jess told us about the big truck I figured he could be compensating for a small—"

"Aaaand we're moving on." Jess rolled her eyes. "He's also well-traveled, been almost anywhere you can think of."

Annette perked up. "Has he been to Funafuti?"

"Funa-whatsis?" Cindy peered at her. "That sounds like a flavor of yogurt."

"It happens to be the capital of Tuvalu."

"Which tells me nothing. Where's that?"

"It's in the South Pacific. I've always wanted to go there. There's a hotel that overlooks the Funafuti lagoon."

"Now I want to go there," Nancy said, "just to say I've been to Funafuti. But we're straying from the topic at hand. I want to know why this handsome, wealthy, well-traveled, well-endowed man is a bit insecure. I'm guessing Desiree has some thoughts."

"He wasn't filthy rich when I knew him, but he had issues. He grew up poor and his father beat the crap out of him. He was afraid to have anything to do with Beau in case he'd repeat that pattern, so he left. He finally came for a short visit after Mav was born."

"That's sad," Annette said, "but he could have come back after Beau was old enough to defend himself. Besides, you wouldn't have let him lay a finger on your son."

She shrugged. "I told him that, and he said his mom hadn't been able to stop his dad."

"But his mom wasn't Desiree McLintock."

Cindy chuckled. "I pity anyone who threatens any of your kids. Or grandkids. I agree he should have shown up long ago, but he probably felt awkward and put it off. The more you put something off, the more awkward it gets. But he's here now, and you said on the phone he proposed?"

"Afraid so. Naturally I turned him down."

"Because you've fallen for Andy?"

"They didn't hear it from me," Jess said. "The whole family is giving them privacy."

"Us, too," Teresa said. "We've been the soul of discretion."

Desiree snorted.

"Well, we have! We haven't teased you or anything. We just teased Andy a little on Christmas Eve."

"And speaking of Andy...." Nancy paused and took a deep breath. "I see what needs to be done. We can't have Jess's father-in-law getting in the way of Jess's father, can we ladies?"

Leave it to Nancy to cut to the chase.

"Sorry, Grandma Dez. Looks like I startled you. Love the name, by the way."

"I admit I thought this discussion would take longer."

"I have inside dope. On the way in I talked with Jess, and she let slip that this meeting was her dad's idea. Andy needs our help. I'm guessing he remembered Teresa's comment from the other night and he wants me, Annette and Teresa to take charge of this guy. Am I right?"

"You are. Also, I'm hoping you'll put him on the road to an attitude adjustment. He can't be a good dad and grandfather if he thinks his worth is tied to his stock portfolio."

"We can work on that, too. Annette? Teresa? You with me?"

Teresa smiled. "I'm in."

"Why not?" Annette lifted her glass. "Here's to saving Steven from himself."

A chorus of save Steven from himself followed.

"Better keep it down." Desiree cocked her head toward the door. "He just drove up."

"I heard that sexy engine rumbling," Teresa said. "I think it's dumb that he bought that truck for no reason other than to show off, but that doesn't mean I wouldn't love a ride in it."

"Then that'll be our first move," Nancy said. "The three of us will ask him to take us for a joyride into town."

"Not just to town." Teresa waggled her eyebrows. "He needs to take us to the Buffalo and buy us each a drink."

"And dance with each of us," Annette said.

"More than once," Nancy added. "And we'll all flirt like crazy."

"Oh, my lord." Colleen couldn't stop laughing. "Can we sneak in and watch?"

Nancy glared at her. "No, you may not. He'll get suspicious if you're all there gawking at us."

Colleen laughed harder. "And he won't get suspicious when three ladies he's never met in his life are treating him like the prize in the box of Cracker Jacks?"

"No, he won't." Nancy lifted her chin. "We'll do it with finesse."

29

Andy was dying to get a report on last night's activities at the Buffalo but Clint had taken the night off and missed the whole show. Rance had been there, but he and a girlfriend went for a sleigh ride this morning and his shift was three to eleven.

He couldn't call Dez to find out what she knew since she was writing. Jess offered to contact Nancy, but he nixed that idea. If Nancy happened to contact Jess, okay, but calling her would be prying.

He'd just have to wait until three and pop over to the Buffalo to see Rance. His version would likely be the best one, anyway. Rance knew how to tell a story.

Then, a little before noon, Jess came into his office, walked over to his desk and leaned down as if she had a secret to tell. "Guess who's here to take you to lunch?"

"Dez?" That would be a nice surprise, but why would Jess be acting like a co-conspirator?

"Steven."

He pushed his glasses to the top of his head and stared at her. "Seriously?"

She kept her voice down. "He's out there right now talking to Joe and Monica."

"Is Beau with him?"

"No, but I suppose he and Mav could be waiting over at the Buffalo."

"Then I guess I'm going to lunch. Wanna come?"

"I wasn't invited. He specifically asked if you were available. Which, come to think of it, tells me Beau and Mav aren't over at the Buffalo or he would have included me. After you leave I'll text Beau and get the 411 on the situation."

He shut down his computer, rolled back his chair and tucked his glasses in his pocket. "Well, I wanted to know what happened last night. Looks like I'll get the story from the horse's mouth."

"Should be fascinating."

"It already is. Was he carrying anything?"

"Like what?"

"A case for a pair of dueling pistols." He unhooked his jacket from the coat tree and grabbed his hat.

She laughed. "He probably left that in his dually."

Stepping close to her, he lowered his voice. "If he offers to give me a ride to the Buffalo, I'm not getting in that truck."

"Why would you? It's two blocks."

"Exactly. I'd never make it to the Buffalo. He'd hit the locks and drive to a place where they'll never find the body."

"That doesn't work anymore, Dad. People have cell phones."

"Keep yours handy. I might need to be rescued."

She kept her back to the door and her voice soft. "If he starts telling war stories about deals he made in Hong Kong, text me an emoji, any emoji. I'll call and say you're desperately needed here."

"Excellent." He motioned her out the door and followed her into the newsroom.

Sure enough, Steven had propped a hip on Joe's desk and was discussing advertising strategies judging from the phrases *good placement* and *capturing eyeballs.* Joe was listening but Monica was only pretending to. He knew that expression.

Andy put on his jovial face. "Hey, Steven, how's it going?"

"Great, Andy." He pushed away from the desk. "Love the historic feel of the building."

"Me, too. Thanks for coming by."

"Figured if I came in person, you'd have a tougher time turning down my invite."

"Nah, I'm a newsman. I can do a face-to-face refusal, no problem. Let's go eat."

"Okay, then." He glanced at Joe and Monica. "Nice meeting you. Nice seeing you again, Jess. The Wenches are a hoot."

"Yes, they are. I'm proud to be one of them."

Andy put on his coat and glanced back at his three musketeers. Best team in the business. "See you guys later. We'll go over the sleigh ride photo layout when I get back."

"Okay, boss man," Monica called after him. Made him smile. She only used that phrase when she thought he needed to lighten up.

Steven held the door for him. "Thanks." He put on his hat. "The Buffalo, I presume?"

"It's still my favorite. I understand Frank's daughter Tyra's running the place, now."

"And doing a bang-up job of it." Andy lengthened his stride, forcing Steven to do the same to keep up with him. Childish, but that Stetson with the bling on it riled up his inner eight-year-old.

"I can tell she's got the touch. Hey, I heard all about that sleigh ride event from the Wenches last night. I ended up making a sizeable donation to the Firehouse Fund."

He managed to hide a grin. "Jess told me about that. They're all extremely impressed with your generosity."

"You know what they say about money. It's like manure. You need to spread it around."

"I've heard that. I also heard that you had something like a triple date last night. How'd that go?"

"Oh, my God, those ladies are so much fun. I like all of 'em, but I really clicked with Nancy."

"Is that so?"

"She's smart and she's sexy. Plus she's a redhead. I really enjoy that combination in a woman." He glanced at Andy. "I figure we're the same in that regard."

"I suppose we are." He'd rather not admit any similarities, but for some reason Steven was buddying up to him. Evidently the Wenches had done exactly what he'd hoped for. Now it was his turn to play along.

Steven asked for a table in the far corner, the most private spot in the place. Curiouser and curiouser.

While Steven scanned the menu, Andy tried not to think of Dez in bed with the guy. Because trying not to think of something always worked so well, of course. He'd better master the trick, though, because chances were good Steven would hang around for a while, unlike Nick, who was currently in Spain.

Spain was a comfortable distance. Sitting on either side of a two-top was an uncomfortable distance. Especially when this former lover had kept his looks. Why couldn't he have gone bald or developed a paunch?

Steven ordered a steak sandwich and a mug of hard cider. He ordered a Reuben and coffee.

Settling back in his chair, Steven gazed at him with eyes the exact color of Beau's, a deep brown. Unnerving. "Guess you can't have booze on a workday. Hope you don't mind if I indulge."

"Absolutely not. I need the caffeine. I'm hoping to finish my New Year's editorial this afternoon. Folks don't always read the editorial, but most of them read this one. I try to make it inspiring."

"I'm sure you succeed."

"Seems like it." He wasn't falling into the trap of false modesty. He was a good writer. Not as good as Dez, but still damned proficient.

"So... about Nancy." Steven rested his forearms on the table and leaned forward. "Like I said, we really got along. When I took them all back to the ranch house, she invited me to follow her over to her place."

"Did she, now?"

"We just talked. For hours. She has a fascinating background in tech. Knows her stuff. But she grew up on a ranch, which is why she bought a place where she could have horses. She took me down to see her barn. Again, nothing happened. I don't want you to get the wrong idea."

"There's no wrong idea, here. You're both consenting adults."

"We are, but... I suppose Desiree told you I offered her a ring."

"She did."

"That's why I wanted to tell you about me and Nancy. I'm not the type to propose to one woman and turn around and take a different one to bed."

"Except Desiree didn't accept your proposal. I think that leaves you free to do whatever you want."

"I suppose, but at this point you know her better than I do. Maybe better than I ever did."

For the first time since Grandpa #2 had pulled in driving that dually, he was genuinely impressed. Humility looked good on the guy. "I guess that's probably true." He added qualifiers on purpose. Now wasn't the time to stake out his territory.

"So do you think she'd lose respect for me if I start dating Nancy? I mean, Desiree will always have a place in my heart, but for now she's chosen you."

He privately flinched at the *for now* part of that sentence, but it was true. They had no commitment.

"The thing is, I'm looking for something stable, basically a place to call home. I felt something tugging at me while I was at Nancy's."

"Was it her goat? I know she has—"

That got a chuckle. "She does. Cute as hell. I meant tugging at my heartstrings. Her place is welcoming. *She's* welcoming. And if it worked out for us, she's not that far from Rowdy Ranch. She mentioned that she rides over sometimes."

Maybe he needed to have a conversation with Nancy to make sure she knew what she was getting into. Then again, Jess said the Wenches had thoroughly discussed Steven's issues before he ever walked into the library.

"You're being quiet over there, Andy. Is this too fast? Will Desiree be upset if Nancy and I become involved?"

"I seriously doubt it." He couldn't wait to see the look on her face when he relayed this conversation. She might be concerned that Nancy had bitten off more than she could chew, but Nancy wasn't an idiot. She'd weigh the pros and cons.

"I assume you'll be seeing her tonight."

"I will."

"It's possible Nancy's talked with her about this. But if you could gauge her reaction and let me know if there's a problem...."

"Be happy to, but if this is what you want and what Nancy wants, I can't imagine Dez being anything but pleased for both of you."

"That's another thing. She doesn't object to you calling her Dez?"

"I sure hope not. I've been doing it for some time, now."

"When I knew her, she was very particular about being called Desiree."

"Well, if she dislikes the nickname, she's never said so, and she's not shy about speaking her mind."

"That's for sure. Somehow her accepting, even liking, that nickname feels significant to me."

"How so?"

"You're the only one who calls her that, which makes you special. It makes your connection deeper, out of the ordinary. As we say in sales, it indicates your relationship has legs. I predict—" He was interrupted when their order arrived.

Andy knew the concept, had even had it applied to the *Sentinel.* Years ago an independent film company had done a documentary on small-town newspapers and had included the *Sentinel.* The narrator had described it as a business that understood its demographic and therefore *had legs*, meaning it would have a long run.

Too bad he didn't share Steven's optimistic view of his relationship with Dez. Her track record wasn't good, and several times she'd warned him to lower his expectations.

The server left, a new kid Clint had just hired. Andy made a mental note to tell Clint he'd hired a winner.

Steven bit into his sandwich and murmured an approval. He finished several bites before he put it down and looked across the table. "Desiree said she'd told you not to propose."

He finished chewing and swallowed. "That's right."

"And you accepted that?"

"It was one of her conditions. Marriage scares her. She thinks she'll end up being dependent on someone."

"You can thank her mother for that. And to some extent, Charley. The two most important people in her life flaked out on her. I didn't help matters, although now I realize she didn't let herself get invested in me."

"Or anyone." He took another bite of his Reuben.

"Evidently. Until you."

He shook his head.

"You don't think so?"

Finishing that bite of sandwich took freaking forever, but he wasn't going to garble this part of the conversation by talking with his mouth full. "She's in love with me, but she's fighting it. She's terrified of becoming dependent on me, on our relationship."

"So you're in limbo."

"Yep."

"I've been in personal limbo for thirty-plus years. I finally decided it sucks. That's why I'm here, why I bought her a ring. Clearly that didn't solve my problem."

Damn it, now he was starting to like the guy. "If it helps any, she wouldn't accept one from me, either."

"Are you sure about that?"

"She flat out told me not to propose. Yeah, I'm sure of that."

"You should have heard how she jumped on me when I said something unflattering about you. She was livid. Told me you were three or four times the man I was."

"Huh."

"She forbid me to ever say anything critical about you again. If I did I'd be out on my ear. I've seen the way she looks at you. She may be fighting her feelings, but she's losing the battle."

"Which could mean she'll eventually call a halt. That worries me." What was he doing? He'd revealed his deepest fear to Dez's ex. What was wrong with him?

"When a client is teetering on the edge like that, I go in with guns blazing."

"And then what?"

"They either show me the door or buy my product, but at least I'm not in limbo."

<u>*30*</u>

Desiree buried herself in her work all day. Steven had texted that he'd be gone most of the day and he'd be at Beau and Jess's for dinner. That meant she was free to unfreeze one of Marybeth's entrees, eat in the kitchen and check messages on her phone.

The one from Andy said he'd arrive at eight, as planned. Nancy's message asked her to call whenever she had time to talk. She tapped Nancy's number.

She answered on the second ring. "I'm so glad you called! I've been dying to tell you about last night."

"Was it fun?"

"We had a blast. He switched off dancing with each of us, which left two of us to dance with each other. We saw glimpses of what you warned us about. He'd find ways to mention how well-off he is. Finally Teresa told him point blank that we didn't care. We weren't gold diggers so he could put a sock in it."

"I love it! Did it work?"

"He struggled at first, but by the time we drove back, it had become a running joke. He'd deliberately brag about his money just to get us all to say *blah, blah, blah.*"

"I'll bet last night was better than ten therapy sessions."

"I think so, too, but that's not the most important thing. He and I hit it off and so when we got back, I asked him to give the three of us a moment to confer. I checked with Teresa and Annette to see whether they'd be upset if I invited him to my place for a nightcap. They were excited for me. They could see there was a spark."

"Wow. This is more than I dared hope for. How did that go?"

"It was fabulous. We talked until three in the morning. He gave me one very chaste kiss although both of us were ramped up. He felt weird taking it further since he just proposed to you, and he—"

"Oh, for goodness sakes. I'll tell him not to get hung up on that. Just make sure you know what you're getting into. One fun night doesn't mean he's fixed."

"I know. I promise to do a gut check every so often, but he fell in love with my place. I think if I invited him to stay here, he would."

"Do you want to? I mean, once a guy's in your house, getting him to leave can be a problem."

"It used to be, but I'm tougher now. If he backslides, I'll do what I need to. I told him I hoped to talk with you, so now I can assure him you're cool with this development."

"Absolutely."

"Then don't wait up for him tonight."

She laughed. "Like I've been doing that."

"I have a good idea what you've been doing. Have fun."

"I will. 'Bye." Now she was impatient for Andy to get here. He'd be tickled with the outcome of his brainstorm.

After cleaning up her dishes and taking Sam out to do his business, she grabbed a quick shower, put on her purple robe and glanced at the clock. Seven-thirty. She settled in the easy chair with her autographed Louis L'Amour book. Maybe he'd be early again.

Instead he was twenty minutes late. She kept checking the clock. Longest twenty minutes ever. When Sam leaped up from his bed and stood waiting at the door, she left her chair and laid down the book.

Had he ever been late in the nearly two years since they'd been brought together by Jess's pregnancy? Not that she could remember. Something must have happened to delay him.

When he walked in, hatless, she took one look at his face and rushed over. "What's wrong? Is it Jess? Mav? Has something—"

"No. Everyone's fine. Sorry I'm late." He handed Sam a treat and clicked the door shut. Then he stared at the key fob in his hand as if he couldn't decide what to do with it. Finally he handed it to her. "Here. You'd better take it for now."

Panic churned in her stomach. "Why? Andy, you're scaring me. Tell me what's the matter."

He let out a sigh. "I'm late because—"

"Hold on. Take off your coat or you'll start sweating."

"Too late." But he took off his coat. He held onto it, though.

Now that she looked more closely, his forehead was shiny with sweat. "Why are you late?"

"I've spent the past half-hour or so parked on the side of the road gearing up for what I need to say."

"About what?" But she could guess. And she didn't want to hear it.

"Us."

Bingo. She steeled herself.

"I haven't been honest with you, Dez. Or honest with myself. I do have an endgame and it's the one you've specifically rejected."

She swallowed. "You want to get married."

"Yes."

"Damn it, Andy. You—"

"I want to be your lover, but I also want to be your husband. I want—"

"This is what I was afraid—"

"I want to go to bed with you at night and wake up with you in the morning, have breakfast, a second cup of coffee, then kiss you and go off to work or off to do errands on Saturday, or sleep in and fool around on Sunday."

She began to shake.

"I realize that in saying this, I'm breaking my promise not to bring up the subject."

"Yes, you are." She cleared her throat. "And I—"

"I'm also indirectly suggesting I move here, which is pushy as hell." He held her gaze. "The thing is, I love you with everything in me. It's a gut-deep feeling and this arrangement doesn't satisfy an essential need I've been ignoring."

"I see." Her words sounded like they'd been run through a shredder.

"Nights in your bed are incredible, but what I really need, what my soul cries out for, is a mutual commitment that we'll love each other for the rest of our lives."

Her chest hurt. Her stomach hurt. Her heart hurt the worst. She took a ragged breath. "But I told you from the beginning...."

"You did. And I lied to you and to myself when I said that was fine, we'd take it one day at a time."

"Andy, I can't give you what you want from me."

Sadness turned his blue eyes gray. "You say can't. I say won't. You've convinced yourself a commitment to me will weaken you."

"Because it will!"

"Not if I can help it. I love that you're strong and capable. I'd celebrate that every single day. I'd be your cheerleader, just like you'd be mine. We'd be stronger together."

"No, we wouldn't because we'd need each other too much. We'd lose the ability to function independently. We'd—"

"That's not what happens, damn it!"

"Yes, it is! When Mary died you were a mess!"

Pain flashed in his eyes.

"I'm sorry. That was mean. I'm sorry."

"I was a mess. But I didn't stay a mess."

"Because Jess came back."

His chest heaved. "Good point. And to that point, okay, if we let ourselves love each other as deeply as I know we can, the person left behind will have a rough time, but—"

"Then you admit it!"

"*But* they will have so many reasons to stay strong, to keep going — the kids, the grandkids, the great-grandkids if we're lucky."

Tears pushed at the back of her eyes. "Why did you have to do this? We were having such a—"

"Great time? Of course we were. And it can continue." He rested his hands on her shoulders and his gaze locked with hers. "Will you marry me, Dez? Please?"

Her stomach churned so violently she was afraid she'd lose her dinner. She could barely force out the word. "No."

"Okay, that's it, then." He left without bothering to put on his coat.

She rushed to the bathroom and threw up everything in her stomach.

31

Andy drove home like a bat out of hell and got stinking drunk. He chose Jack Daniel's because it was quicker than beer. He didn't need as much booze to get smashed as he used to, so it didn't take long before he was passed out on his sofa.

He woke up around three hating life. He was too old for this nonsense. He should have made himself a cup of hot chocolate instead. Then he cursed that thought to hell and back.

Guaranteed Dez had ruined him for having sex with anyone else. She'd also ruined him for any hot chocolate except hers. And last but not least, she'd broken his heart into a million pieces. He could hear it rattling around in there.

He wanted to blame Steven effing Jacobson for this fustercluck. God, how he wanted to lay the blame on her ex's gold-plated doorstep.

But he couldn't. Steven had simply pointed out what he hadn't wanted to acknowledge. She'd told him the truth while they sat at her kitchen table last Friday afternoon. He was the marrying kind.

He'd done his best to transform into the secret lover kind who crept into her bed in the dead of night and stole away before dawn. Turned out he was lousy at the secret lover gig. He'd lasted less than a week before blowing up the program.

Heading for the bathroom, he stripped down and stood under a hot shower until it turned cold. Then he toweled off, took two aspirin, set his alarm and crawled into bed.

Big surprise, sleep wouldn't come. Was she in the same shape? If only he didn't care. But he did. He loved her and that was that. They were perfect for each other in every way except this one thing. This one big thing.

Yeah, she wasn't sleeping, either. He'd bet on it. And it was his fault. No, not just his fault. They'd created this situation together, each fooling themselves that it would work.

Finally he threw back the covers and got out of bed. Where was his phone? He walked through the dark house without turning on lights because he couldn't remember if he'd pulled down the shades. Consequently he stubbed his toe. Twice.

A shaft of moonlight through the living room window fell on the coffee table, reflecting off the screen of his phone. No, he hadn't pulled the shades, so good thing he hadn't turned on a lamp and flashed any insomniac neighbors.

His phone lit up and pinged. His pathetic heart started pounding like the feet of an Irish step-dancer.

Her text was short. *I'm so sorry.*
He typed a reply. *Me, too.*
Let's not tell the kids.
They'll figure it out.

Maybe not right away.

I won't say anything. But when he appeared in the office looking like a cast member from *The Walking Dead*, Jess would notice. She was his daughter and a trained journalist. Nothing got by her.

I won't say anything, either. Don't forget we have the New Year's Eve party at the Buffalo Sunday night.

Like he would forget. As he'd sunk into his Jack Daniel's induced stupor, he'd contemplated the likelihood of pulling off a happy Andy act on New Year's Eve and a jolly Grandy act on New Year's Day when the family gathered in Rowdy Roost. He didn't have high hopes.

But he typed what he thought she wanted to hear. *It'll be fine.* He seriously doubted that, but what was he supposed to say? That it would be an unmitigated disaster?

I didn't get to tell you about Nancy and Steven.

That's okay. Steven told me.

When?

He took me to lunch.

To talk about Nancy?

And you. He didn't want you to be upset.

I'm not.

I told him you wouldn't be.

It would be nice if it works out.

Yep. Then the irony of it hit him. His plan had provided Steven with a potential romance while his had gone down in flames.

I should let you get some sleep.

No worries. I wasn't having much luck with that. He didn't count passing out as actual sleep. More like anesthetizing himself against the pain.

Me, either.

Is Sam sleeping?

Not really.

Tell Sam I'm sorry.

I will. He'll miss you.

I'll miss him.

Good night, Andy.

Good night, Dez. He held the phone for several minutes in case she thought of something else to say. Like maybe *I'll miss you.*

She would. He knew that for a fact. She'd missed him so much last Sunday that she'd canceled his nighttime visit out of fear she was becoming dependent.

If she missed him even more now, she'd likely take that as proof that loving him was a bad thing that would make her weak. Would she try to stop loving him?

If she succeeded in that, he'd need to find out how she accomplished it. As it stood, he couldn't imagine that he'd ever stop loving her. She had his heart, whether she wanted it or not, until it stopped beating.

* * *

Having a work-in-progress could be a blessing or a curse. When interesting activities tempted Desiree to ignore her deadline, it was a curse. But when life had knocked her sideways and she desperately needed to escape, it was a blessing.

She could tell her kids that A) she'd hit a rough spot in the book and she had to keep at it until she punched through the problem, or B) her characters were talking to her, the story was rolling like a movie in her head and she didn't dare interrupt the flow.

At eight in the morning after a disastrous night, she sent a joint text to her family and the Wenches citing Option B as the reason she'd be out of touch until the party on New Year's Eve. No one should need her for anything. She had no responsibility for the Bash at the Buffalo as they'd started calling it. The gang would gather in Rowdy Roost on New Year's Day, but that was traditionally a potluck.

Ironically, her story *was* flowing. How that was possible was a mystery even Andy wouldn't have been able to solve. The minute she stepped away from her desk, misery swamped her. Tears dribbled down her cheeks and she ached all over.

Missing Andy was a wound that wouldn't heal, a gaping hole in her life that nothing would ever fill. She wanted him there so she could shout at him. *See? This is what happens! The pain is beyond enduring!*

Except when she sat down at the keyboard and lost herself in the story, she was fine. Thank God. If breaking up with Andy had torpedoed her work... but it hadn't. Evidently she'd created a protective shield around her creativity. That was reassuring. She'd survive this.

On Saturday morning when she was in the kitchen fetching more coffee, Sam raced to the door at the sound of a truck. Then the New Year's edition of the *Sentinel* hit the front porch.

A premonition sent her racing to the window, heart thumping. Sure enough, Andy was pulling away.

Gasping for breath, she fogged up the window. She quickly wiped it with the sleeve of her purple robe. He was gone. She paid extra for home delivery — all the kids did, too — and normally a high school student made the trip out to the rural subscribers.

Would any of her family members notice Andy had delivered the paper? Likely not. She wouldn't have if she hadn't chosen this moment to grab more coffee.

She was alone in the house except for Sam. Marybeth typically took Saturday and Sunday mornings off to tend things in her own house. Steven had moved his stuff over to Nancy's place.

She went to open the front door. The cold morning air felt good on her hot cheeks. A glimpse of his truck was all she'd needed to be filled with hot waves of yearning.

The paper lay exactly in front of it, held together with a rubber band as usual. When the high schoolers made the delivery, it often ended up in the yard or the bushes. But Andy's toss was dead center.

Sam trotted outside and looked around, tail wagging.

"I doubt he's coming back, Sam. Might as well get the paper and come inside where it's warm."

He glanced back at her, then gazed longingly at the empty road.

"I know just how you feel, puppy-dog."

With a sigh that fogged the air, he picked up the paper in his teeth and brought it to her.

"Thanks." She took a cookie from her pocket and traded it for the paper. He headed off to the kitchen and his bed.

Closing the door, she followed him, intending to leave the paper on the table, pick up her coffee and go back to her office. Except maybe Andy had tucked a note inside the paper.

Pulling off the rubber band, she unfolded the edition. The front page featured a large picture of the sleigh headed down Main Street. She took her glasses out of her bathrobe pocket. Beau was driving it, with Kendall, Cheyenne, Jodie, Zach and Mav as his passengers.

More pictures occupied the two-page centerfold. She studied them all, pride swelling in her chest. Her kids had organized a worthwhile project and the town had supported it, especially the *Sentinel* and its owner. This edition would be a keeper.

Andy's editorial occupied its normal place on the second page, the first thing she normally turned to. She shouldn't read it now. Maybe she shouldn't read it ever.

But he'd personally delivered the paper. He didn't do things for no reason. He hadn't left a note, but he had written the editorial.

Taking her coffee to the table, she slid into a chair and spread the paper in front of her. Just like reading the texts he'd sent in the wee hours

Thursday morning, she'd hear his voice as she read the editorial.

That would be tough, but she'd better get used to communicating with him without freaking out. They'd be seeing each other tomorrow night at the Buffalo and they couldn't act like strangers.

She took a sip of coffee, then drew a shaky breath and began to read.

Howdy, folks. It's that time again. Here we are, teetering on the edge between one year and the next, looking back at what's in the past and forward to what will happen in the future. If you're like me, you've had triumphs and tribulations, and with luck the triumphs were in the lead.

Not every life event weighs the same, though. The triumph of your checking account figures matching your bank statement to the penny won't make up for the time your phone fell out of your pocket and you ran over it with your truck. Not that I'm familiar with that scenario.

In the grand scheme of things, though, neither of those events are life-changing. Let's suppose that in this past year, when the chips were down, you took a huge risk and shoved all your chips to the center of the table? For one shining moment, you're Rooster Cogburn riding with the reins in your teeth, guns blazing.

But instead of winning the day, you end up like Wile E. Coyote, flattened by a boulder. That's a big deal tribulation right there. Probably outweighs all the triumphs you can scrape together. Do you learn your lesson and vow never to take that kind of risk again?

I hope not. Wile E. doesn't. Before long he's back at it, optimistic that next time, things will be different. In Wile E.'s case it's not, poor sucker.

That said, I love the part where he goes from flat as a pancake to fully-formed Wile E. It's resilience at its finest.

That's the spirit in which I approach every New Year's Eve. We flip the calendar and go from flat-Wile E. to reconstituted Wile E. And if you feel the urge to shove all your chips into the center of the table in the New Year, go for it. Even if you get flattened by a boulder, you won't stay that way. Just ask Wile E. Or me.

Happy New Year,
Andy

_32_

The Bash at the Buffalo wouldn't provide Andy with any protective coloring. He couldn't slide into Grandy mode tonight since Buck and Marybeth were keeping Mav, Jodie and Susie, while Mrs. J, Molly's grandmother, had Zach and Elvira.

Normally he liked to arrive at a New Year's Eve party on the late side so he didn't run out of steam before midnight. and it was doubly true this time. He felt no urgency to be there before eleven, but he would show up, by God.

He'd received the group text on Thursday morning along with everyone else. Dez had retreated into her writing cave and would emerge for the Bash at the Buffalo. Nice strategy that hadn't been available to him.

Instead he'd faked coming down with a winter cold. He must have sounded convincing on the phone with Jess early Thursday morning because she'd brought him leftover chicken soup on her way into the newsroom.

He'd been a little afraid to eat it since Marybeth's recipe was supposed to foster trust and he was lying through his teeth. Not being physically in his office hadn't been a problem, though. He'd emailed his column to Monica and pretended to everyone he was still highly contagious and was resting and drinking fluids so he could make it to the Bash Sunday night.

He'd taken a chance coming out of hiding to deliver the papers to Rowdy Ranch. He'd contacted his delivery kid and asked him to drop that particular batch at his house.

Fortunately he'd had no phone calls or texts mentioning his paperboy gig, so nobody had seen him do it. He'd heard stories about the *Sentinel* going astray in the bushes and he couldn't let that happen with Dez's copy.

He'd written the editorial as a reminder to himself, a gut check about who he was and what he stood for. In the process, he needed to let her know, in print because that was their medium of choice, that she hadn't left him a hollow shell of a man.

Well, she had, temporarily. Recovery from her rejection had been slower than he would have liked. His batteries weren't completely recharged, but he was getting there.

He couldn't look forward to nights in her bed, but he wasn't in limbo, either. When it came to Dez, things couldn't get worse, which meant they could only get better.

Had she read his editorial? He wouldn't count on it. She might read it next week or never. Tonight he'd greet her as a treasured friend and family member.

The Buffalo must be packed to the gills. He had to leave his truck three blocks away. As he walked back to the entrance, he scanned the row of vehicles. No BPT, her acronym for Big Purple Truck.

Had she decided to skip the event or maybe left early? That would suck. He wanted to face her, have a nice conversation, start rebuilding whatever relationship they'd have going forward.

She could have ridden in with one of the kids. That actually made sense. If she was in the mood to tie one on, and she very well might be, she shouldn't be driving home.

Opening the door confirmed that the Buffalo was a madhouse. Between the band and the partiers, he could barely hear the buffalo moan *Haaaappyyyy Froliiiicking' Neeeew Yeeeaarrr!*

Clint and Tyra had set an age limit of twenty-one and over since it was a late-night party that wasn't designed for kids. Instead the room was full of adults acting like kids.

Flashing headbands and necklaces were everywhere, as well as noisemakers that unfurled when you blew into them. Line dancers crowded the floor as the band blasted Brad Paisley's *Welcome to the Future.*

He took off his coat and hat while scanning the room for Dez. He'd covered about a third of the crowd when Steven showed up, his arm around Nancy's shoulders. They looked good together. She'd worn her gold dress and Steven had on a Western-styled vest with gold thread running through it, as if they'd planned to coordinate.

"Hey, you two, how's it going?"

"We're having fun." Nancy gazed up at Steven. "At least I am."

"Me, too. Big fun." Steven gave her an appreciative smile before turning his attention back to Andy. "Kind of late, aren't you?"

"I like coming in about now. Then I don't run out of steam before midnight."

"Fair enough. Good editorial, by the way. I'll bet you took that *teetering on the edge* phrase from our conversation the other day."

"I did. Memorable phrase. Stuck in my head. I'll be happy to split the royalties with you."

"You get royalties for that?"

"No, but if it goes viral, and somebody wants to license that paragraph and put it on a T-shirt, we can split the proceeds."

"You're kidding, but you never know. It could happen."

Nancy gave him a hip bump. "But if it does, the money's not important, right, Steve?"

He laughed. "Money's *always* important."

"Blah, blah, blah." She grinned at him.

He grinned right back, then glanced at Andy. "It's our little joke."

Fascinating. It might be partly that the guy was slightly toasted, but he didn't act at all like the person who'd driven up to Beau and Jess's place in the dually. The Wenches, and specifically Nancy, deserved a medal.

"Speaking of teetering on the edge," Steven — now Steve — pointed to a far corner of the room. "Desiree's over there."

"Thanks. I was wondering. I didn't see her truck out front."

"She rode in with Beau and Jess. She's drinking hot cider, the hard version. Looked like she could use a refill."

"Then I'll bring her one."

Nancy skewered him with a look. "She was asking about you earlier, wondered if you'd recovered from your cold."

"She knew about my cold?"

"Well, duh. We all knew about your cold. And her writing binge. What a coincidence that you were both out of pocket at the same time, huh?"

"Life's a mystery." But not to this family or the Wenches. They knew something was up. He'd been afraid of that. "I'd better go get her that cider before she orders one herself."

Nancy gave a nod of approval. "You should."

He walked over to the bar and Clint happened to be the one to fill his cider. When he pulled cash from his wallet, Clint waved it away.

"Your money's no good here, Andy."

"C'mon. Everybody else pays. You can't afford to give the whole family free drinks."

"But you said it was for Mom, and chances are it's a peace offering."

"A peace offering? No, it's just—"

"Take it with my blessing. Glad you made it. We were all a little worried you might not. We're pulling for you, dude."

Andy groaned. "Are there no secrets in this family?"

"Plenty, but your struggle with Mom is not one of them. Look, we all know her. We know what you're up against. We want you to keep trying."

"What if she doesn't want that?"

Clint took a couple of seconds before he responded. "Just between you and me."

"Absolutely."

"My mother is so smart about everything except… well, this issue. Don't give up on her. Please."

He sucked in a breath. "Okay."

"Let me have your stuff. You need to be unencumbered."

That made him laugh, but he obligingly handed his coat and hat across the bar. "Normally I leave everything at whatever table we've staked out, but—"

"Operation central for our gang is on the far side of the room, but you don't have to drag your coat and hat over there. This is fine. Good luck."

"Thanks." He turned and headed through the crowd. Yeah, he was in love with the whole damn family. Maybe he should just move into the barn and wait the lady out, one day at a time. Her kids would likely bring him food.

The trip across the room took forever, but then he found Beau and Jess, who greeted him enthusiastically and stepped aside, putting him face-to-face with Dez. If she'd had a mug of cider, she'd left it somewhere.

She beamed at him. "You finally made it."

"Yes, ma'am." That warm smile threw him off his game. No flicker of anxiety, no hitch in her breathing. Who would guess she'd been shouting at him four nights ago?

She was poised, elegant, and so beautiful. Her purple silk blouse was tucked into the slim waist of her long black skirt with a slit up one side to reveal sleek black boots. Sparkles in her hair added a festive touch. Maybe he could be forgiven for staring.

"Is that for me or you?"

"You." He handed it to her. "You look terrific, Dez."

"Thank you. Where's your drink?"

"Still in the vat since I didn't want to risk battling this throng with two full mugs."

Jess rested her hand on his shoulder. "Is your cold better, Dad?"

"Way better." He smiled at her. "Thanks for the chicken soup. It did the trick."

"I was gettin' worried, Andy," Beau said. "If you hadn't shown up soon, I was gonna drive over and roust you out."

"I tried to convince Beau you liked to come to these late," Jess said. "You did the same last year."

"But I didn't remember that, probably because I was focused on whether Mav was okay since we weren't used to leaving her."

"I didn't remember either, Beau. I was worried, too." She set her mug on a nearby table. "Hey, will you watch that for me while Andy and I mosey over to the bar and fetch his drink?"

"Sure thing, Mom."

Promising suggestion. He'd wander anywhere she cared to go.

She glanced at Jess and Beau. "We'll be back in a bit."

"Don't take too long." Jess checked the large clock on the wall. "Only twenty minutes until midnight."

"That should be enough time."

He looked at her. "For what?"

She just smiled, tilted her head toward the bar and led the way.

He followed and the return trip was easier. Folks tended to step back and let her through because she was Desiree McLintock.

Clint grinned when he spotted them. "I see you found each other."

"We did, son. Is Tyra in the office?"

"No, she's schmoozing with the customers. She loves this New Year's Eve party."

"I figured she wouldn't be back there this time of night. Is it locked?"

"Yes, ma'am. Would you like the key?"

"I would."

Andy gave her a startled glance.

"We'll pick up your cider on the way back." She gestured toward the revelers. "We need to get out of this hullabaloo. I have some things I want to say and you can't hear yourself think out here."

Something to say? What the hell did that mean? His chest tightened.

Clint slid the keyring across the bar and Dez picked it up. "Thanks." She started toward the back of the building.

Andy glanced at Clint and shrugged.

Clint gave him a thumbs up.

Maybe the guy knew something he didn't. Heading after her, he lengthened his stride. "Does this have anything to do with my editorial?"

"It does."

"What did you think?"

"I'll tell you in a minute." She walked fast, her boot heels clicking on the wood floor. Stopping in front of a plain paneled door, she inserted the key and opened it.

"I don't think I've ever been back here."

"It's not exactly loaded with atmosphere." She flicked on an overhead light. "But it's warm, relatively quiet and we won't be disturbed." She walked in. "Let's each take a chair."

There went his fantasy that she'd grab him the minute they were alone. He closed the door, muffling the noise of the party. The small office had two desks back-to-back facing opposite walls. Two oak swivel desk chairs on rollers occupied most of the space in the middle.

Dez took one and he took the other, turning it so he faced her, his knees almost touching hers. "Lay it on me."

Resting her arms on the arms of the chair, she looked almost relaxed. Almost. A bright gleam in her hazel eyes and a slight tension in her jaw indicated plenty was going on in her head. "I read your editorial."

"When?"

"Right after you delivered it."

"You saw me?"

"Sam alerted me. You have good aim, by the way."

"Thanks."

"Since you personally delivered it and made sure it didn't end up in the bushes, I gathered that you wanted to be sure I read it."

"Or at least be sure you'd have the chance to. If you cared to." He drew in a breath, mirroring her almost-calm posture. Good sign that she'd read it right away.

She gave him a once-over. "You look reconstituted on the outside. How about the inside? No fibbing. I don't believe your winter cold story for a minute."

"I had a rough couple of days. Composing the editorial helped. I guess you could say I wrote myself out of the worst of it." He paused. "How about you? How's the book coming along? No fibbing."

"That's the weird part. The writing's going great. Thursday and Friday, the only time I felt halfway human was when I was working on it. The minute I stopped, I was a mess."

He winced. "Sorry."

"You have nothing to be sorry for. You did what you had to do. If it put me in a tailspin, that's my problem, not yours."

"Easy to say, but I love you. When you hurt, I hurt. That's how it works."

She breathed in slowly and let it out just as slowly. "I know. You were part of the reason I was such a mess for the first couple of days. I knew you were miserable."

"But you got better?"

"I did. Especially after I read your editorial. I heard your voice in my head. You were bravely working through this, which I found inspiring. And then... then it came to me."

He sat up straighter. Her voice had a quiver. A faint one, but he was listening very hard and he caught it.

"You said we'd be stronger together, not weaker." She swallowed. "I didn't get it, then, but now I do. We were suffering at the same time, calling on our reserves, doing our work. It may sound dorky, but our coping strategies are so much alike that it became a bonding thing."

He held his breath.

"That editorial was your hand reaching out to take mine, not to prop me up, but to reconnect to let me know you understand."

"Yes."

"You gave me hope we can work this out with the help of... our love for each other."

He left his chair and pulled her out of hers. "Thank God, Dez." He wrapped her in his arms, his throat so tight he could barely choke out the words. "Thank God."

Tears glistened in her eyes. "I want you to move to the ranch."

Joy flooded through him. It wasn't a proposal. But it was a beginning. "I—"

"That's only if you want to. It's a long drive to the office, but—"

"I don't give a damn. I'll start packing."

"We'll take it slow. You've lived in that house a long time."

"And you've lived alone for a long time."

"I want you there. The way you handled the past few days tells me it will work. But I don't want to wrench you away from an environment you cherish."

"Wrench me away, lady. Nothing in that house is more important than you."

"Maybe we could add on, build you an office on the other side of my bedroom."

"But we can't get rid of the secret door. I love that door."

She smiled and swiped at her eyes. "We'll talk about it. We'll talk about everything."

"I'm ready to stop talking and start kissing." As he leaned down, someone rapped hard on the door.

"Three minutes to midnight, guys!" Clint called out.

He gazed at her. "Do you care?"

"Yes. We need to get out there."

"Why? I guarantee we'll hear the countdown and I can kiss you a lot better in here."

"I want to share this with everyone." She wiggled out of his arms. "Come on."

"This? The fact I'm moving to the ranch?"

"Just go with it." Grabbing his hand, she opened the door and tugged him into the hallway. She paused long enough to lock the door and then handed him the key. "I don't have pockets."

He shoved it in his jeans pocket and hurried with her out past the bar. The band had stopped playing. Clint and Rance had abandoned their posts to be with the family.

Once again, Dez was the magic ticket when it came to navigating through the crowd to the far side of the room. They made it to the McLintocks for the countdown.

Ten! Nine! Eight! Seven! Six! Five! Four! Three! Two! One! Happy New Year!

As the band played a country version of *Auld Lang Syne,* Andy finally claimed the kiss he'd been yearning for, the one he'd feared might never happen.

She kissed him back. Oh, did she kiss him back. She was all in, and he suspected the cheers he was hearing in the group surrounding them were no longer about New Year's.

Finally decency required he end it. They had all night. He wouldn't be sneaking out before dawn this time. Slowly he lifted his head. "Happy New Year, Dez."

She gazed up at him, her face flushed, her eyes shining. "Happy New Year, Andy. Will you marry me?"

He gaped at her. "What?"

"You heard me." She spoke a little louder. "Andy Hartmann, will you marry me?"

The McLintock family stopped cheering and singing. The band continued to play *Auld Lang Syne* and the rest of the crowd sang along, but this bunch went dead silent.

He stared at her in disbelief. "Do you mean it?"

"Of course I mean it. I love you and I want to marry you. What do you say?"

"*Hell, yeah!*" It came out as a triumphant roar. When he scooped her up and swung her around, their beloved family went crazy.

Someone, probably Beau, shouted *Mom and Andy are getting married!* and the entire room abandoned *Auld Lang Syne* to add their cheers, applause and whistles. The noise was deafening.

Dez gazed at him with her million-watt smile. "See what you made me do?"

"Uh-huh. Let's see how they react if I kiss you again."

"I don't think they can get much louder."

But they did. As his lips touched down on hers, the hooting and hollering rivaled the sound of a cattle stampede. The band's drummer added to it.

She started laughing and so did he. He gave up on the kiss and simply looked at her, no doubt with a goofy smile on his face that exactly matched hers.

Maybe it was fitting that this moment had caused such a ruckus. Against all odds, Desiree Annabelle McLintock was getting married. And wonder of wonders, she'd chosen him.

New York Times bestselling author Vicki Lewis Thompson's love affair with cowboys started with the Lone Ranger, continued through Maverick, and took a turn south of the border with Zorro. She views cowboys as the Western version of knights in shining armor, rugged men who value honor, honesty and hard work. Fortunately for her, she lives in the Arizona desert, where broad-shouldered, lean-hipped cowboys abound. Blessed with such an abundance of inspiration, she only hopes that she can do them justice.

For more information about this prolific author, visit her website and sign up for her newsletter. She loves connecting with readers.

VickiLewisThompson.com

Milton Keynes UK
Ingram Content Group UK Ltd.
UKHW011041201123
432908UK00005BA/580